THE MYSTERY OF RUBY'S PORT

ROSE DONOVAN

Moon Snail Press

For Seva

MORE RUBY DOVE MYSTERIES

Sign up for email updates and bonus material. Details can be found at the end of *The Mystery of Ruby's Port*.

Cast of Characters on the SS Sanguine

Ruby Dove – Student of chemistry at Oxford, fashion designer and amateur spy-sleuth. Assistant to Gustave Marchand on this ill-fated voyage.

Fina Aubrey-Havelock – Student of history at Oxford, assistant seamstress to Ruby and her best friend. Governess to Victor Winchcombe-Twisleton on this cruise to disaster.

Ian Clavering – Theatre producer, smashing fashion plate, and a follower of Ruby.

Lev Nesterov – Steward with a taste for cocktails and political intrigue.

Agnes Gidge – Artist, gossiper and maid.

Sarah Breeze – Poet and on-board cook.

Balraj Chadha – Film star and life of the party.

Lady Winchcombe-Twisleton, née Sadie Stiles – Mother of Victor and widow of Lord Winchcombe-Twisleton. A social climber.

Victor Winchcombe-Twisleton – Son of Sadie Stiles. A swine enthusiast.

Gustave Marchand – Fashion designer from Paris with a rather vague past.

Neville Emmanuel Raymond – Steward who appreciates mystery books and Fina Aubrey-Havelock.

Maxwell Mills – Captain of the SS *Sanguine*. Ian's old school chum.

Dolores Dominguez – Hollywood star. Has little tolerance for antics of others.

Patricia Burbage – Sister to Emeline. Superstitious heir to oil company fortune.

Emeline Caulk – Sister to Patricia. Missionary.

Phillip Gibbs – Father to Gilbert and husband of Violet. Plenty of energy, nervous or otherwise.

Violet Gibbs – Mother to Gilbert and wife to Phillip. An unhappy traveller.

Gilbert Gibbs – Son of Phillip and Violet. A mischief-maker when he gets the chance.

Souse – Head cat of the SS *Sanguine* with a taste for Sarah Breeze's cooking.

1
___

A white object fluttered down into the blue of the sea.

Clutching her hat and stomach at the same time, Fina leaned over the railing. The booklet had fallen face down, gently skimming the water's surface on a journey into the unknown.

"Ruby!" shrieked Fina, leaning so far over the gangplank railing that she risked meeting the same fate as her passport.

Ruby, positioned below Fina on the dock, sprang into action. As she slid with a fluid movement to her left, she snatched an oar from a nearby rowing boat. She plied it into the water and scooped up the soggy miscreant.

As Ruby lifted her prize up in triumph, Fina saw her friend nearly drop both the oar and the passport into the water. Ruby craned her neck to the side, her face now displaying a round "O" of surprise.

Fina leaned over the railing even further to glimpse who or what had surprised her friend. Seeing nothing, she let out a sigh of relief that her passport was safe.

It was not an auspicious way to start their journey from Nassau, in the Bahamas, to Trinidad's Port of Spain. Knowing that Ruby would soon join her on deck, with not long to wait before the ship set off, Fina strolled up the gangplank, onto the SS *Sanguine*.

It was a glorious day, though Fina realised that most days in Nassau were probably glorious, especially compared to the grey of Oxford. She admired the graceful lines of the SS *Sanguine*, and felt a surge of pleasurable anticipation of their voyage.

"Pardon me!"

A surge of pain replaced that of anticipation as large suitcase rammed into her legs, nearly knocking Fina overboard like her passport. Turning to see the source of the pain, she saw two tall figures striding along the deck away from her.

Hmph, thought Fina. How positively rude.

The tallest figure, encased in a rather unseasonable tweed, spat out, "Young ladies," as if describing a troublesome slug found in the garden. The shorter figure – though still quite tall – clad in a fashionable yachting outfit, replied, "Come along, Emmy. I do hope our cabin isn't as dreadful as the one on our voyage from Southampton."

Fina turned back toward the gangplank, wincing as she rubbed the back of her leg. Thank goodness that pair hadn't been aboard the same ship as she and Ruby had taken from Southampton themselves.

A small child in white, perhaps aged five, skipped up the gangplank. He held a toy ship aloft, flying it as if it were an airplane. "Mummy! Mummy, can I have the lolly we brought with us now?" he enquired, turning back to a woman in a faded, flowered frock. The woman grasped the rope and pulled herself up toward the deck, reminding Fina of the last few steps of a mountain climber before she reaches the summit.

"Not at the moment, Gilbert," she gasped, letting out a great stream of air as she dropped a small but apparently stupendously heavy bag onto the deck.

"Let's not bother Mummy right now, Gilbert. Come along.

Let's help Mummy carry her bag," said a genial-looking man in a rather shabby brown suit more suitable to Brighton than the Bahamas. He gave Fina a slight nod and a smile by way of introduction and then continued on his way down the deck, toward the cabins. His wife also gave Fina a smile, though it was rather wan. She could see little beads of sweat along the woman's hairline as she dragged herself after her son and husband. Was she ill? Were they on holiday?

A tug on her sleeve jolted Fina's naturally inquisitive and wandering mind. Looking down – though not too far given her small stature – she saw the red head of Victor Winchcombe-Twisleton. Victor's eyes peered up at her through round, rather adorable tortoiseshell glasses. "Would you read this to me, Miss Aubrey-Havelock?" he enquired while proffering a book titled *Little Grey Rabbit*.

Shading her eyes from the sun, Fina squinted at him and said, "I'd be delighted to, Victor, but you can read it yourself! How about you read it to me?"

"Not now, Victor," rumbled a silky yet slightly gravelly voice. "Leave Miss Aubrey-Havelock alone. I'm sure she's just dying to get to her room." Fina gave the speaker a grateful nod. "Thank you, Lady Winchcombe-Twisleton—" said Fina.

"Please just call me Sadie, Miss Aubrey-Havelock."

"Sadie, then. And please do call me Fina. I was about to suggest that I come to your cabin once we get settled – if that agrees with you – and we'll discuss which lessons you'd like me to go over with Victor during the voyage. Then perhaps the two of us can explore the ship together," she said, giving Victor a light touch on the shoulder. He grinned.

"That sounds like a smashing idea, as you Brits say," said Lady Winchcombe-Twisleton with a wave of her hand, which caused her emerald green satin frock to ripple from the movement. Fina watched as she sauntered off with Victor and a porter in tow. Marvellous confidence, sighed Fina to herself. You would never think she had been born plain old Sadie Stiles.

"Mooooo," the ship boomed. Clearly an All Aboard signal. Fina felt that familiar anxious knot settle in her stomach. She ran to the side of the ship and yelled, "Ruby!"

No one answered.

2

———

"Feens, don't worry – I'm here."

Fina spun round and saw her friend, resplendent in her signature grey travelling outfit – though this time it was in a more appropriate linen rather than wool – leaning on the railing. She held up Fina's passport by one corner, as if it had an unpleasing odour.

"I'm afraid it is rather waterlogged, but it will soon dry in this lovely warm sun."

Claiming the passport with a sheepish smile, Fina said, "Thank you! You've saved my bacon – again. But how did you find your way on board? I've been on deck the whole time, waiting for you."

"Well, there is another way. You'll never guess who showed it to me. Never."

"Out with it!" squealed Fina.

A deep, lilting voice boomed out from further down the deck. "It was me."

Fina clutched the railing. "Ian! What on earth are you doing aboard?" Ian Clavering, clad in a white suit and red cravat, looked as dashing as ever. The navy blue square peeking out of his pocket was an impeccable final touch, she thought.

Ian's eyebrows wriggled as he gave out a short laugh. "Following you two, of course."

"No, but quite seriously, what are you doing on board?" Fina queried.

"Well, as I told Ruby a minute ago, it's more plausible to ask that question of you two. After all, I'm from the Bahamas, remember?"

Indeed she did. How could she forget this man who had figured so prominently in the mysterious affair at Pauncefort Hall last winter? Casting her mind back, she could almost hear the voice of Lady Charlotte, pointing out Ian to her and explaining that even though he was one of London's top theatre producers, he often spent half the year in the Bahamas to be with his family. She had wondered at the time how he managed it.

Ruby intervened. "Ian doesn't read *Drapers Record* as faithfully as you and I do, Feens, so he won't have heard of Gustave Marchand. I had to explain to him that I was accompanying an aspiring new dress designer, whose ambitions are the talk of Paris. He is keen to meet Trinidadian designers and talk to them about developing his first full collection."

"After all the expert sleuthing you two did at Pauncefort Hall, I'd almost forgotten about your second career as tailoresses," remarked Ian.

Ruby's arched eyebrows showed what she thought of his choice of words, but she let it pass. In the interest of harmony, Fina jumped in.

"When I found out about Ruby's opportunity, I tried to figure out a way to tag along," she said, turning toward Ian. "It seemed rather dire as I scarcely have a shilling to my name, but Mr

Marchand was kind enough to contact Lady Winchcombe-Twisleton. She is an American who married the late Lord Winchcombe-Twisleton. You might have read about his untimely death – about a year ago – in the newspapers. She is determined to raise her son, Victor, in England. Mr Marchand asked her if I could be governess to Victor on this trip, as a sort of test run to continue on when we return to London. But I'm babbling on – you must be ready to settle into your cabin."

"That's kind of you, Fina. I've actually already settled in. The captain of the ship, Maxwell Mills, is an old school friend of mine. I've been on board a few days already."

"Oh. Is that why you're here – to reminisce with an old friend?" asked Fina.

Ian's eyelids flickered. "Yes, partially." He cleared his throat. "I have some business contacts in Port of Spain, so I thought I'd combine business with pleasure," he said, eyeing Ruby. "Little did I know how much pleasure until you two showed up."

Ruby did not appear impressed. Fina was puzzled. She expected her friend to be pleased, or at least to display a nervous energy, given how sparks had flown between her and Ian when they were at Pauncefort Hall.

"Yes, well, we'll see you around, Ian," said Ruby in a flat voice. With that, she turned toward the starboard side of the ship and began to walk with purpose toward what must be their cabin.

Feeling slightly embarrassed by Ruby's rather uncharacteristically abrupt behaviour – usually that was her own calling card – Fina gave Ian an apologetic little smile and scurried off after her friend.

She hurried along the deck, admiring the gently rocking boats in the harbour. Even though she skidded down the deck in haste, she savoured the pungent smell of the sea.

Snap.

Her handbag slid across the planks as she tripped on a rope lying across the deck. "Selkies and kelpies," she muttered to herself. Out of the ether, a youngish man, perhaps in his early thirties, materialised. He wore a charming striped sailor's shirt. "*Vybachte* – I'm sorry," he said in a clipped voice. His face looked more apologetic than his words conveyed. He held out a hand to Fina.

"My name is Lev, Lev Nesterov. Steward and deckhand. Please forgive my rope. I think all passengers are in their cabins – so I do some deck work," he said, rubbing the leg of his trouser nervously with his other leg.

"Pleased to meet you, Lev. My name is Fina."

"You do not go by Miss So-and-so? That is a relief," he said. He held his hand to his mouth as if he was appalled by his own words.

With a burbling laugh, Fina replied, "Yes, please do call me Fina. I'm working as a governess for Lady Winchcombe-Twisleton."

The ship gave a great lurch as it prepared to leave the harbour. Lev reached out to steady Fina.

"Yes," he said. "We will all need to get our – it is what in English? Sea legs. Yes. So you must be in cabin number I, next to Lady Twisleton-Winchcombe... I mean Twislecombe-Winchton. Ah!" he said, holding his hands aloft in frustration. "You know what I mean. Here, I will assist you."

Lev guided Fina down the gleaming beige wooden deck toward her cabin. After thanking him and providing a small tip – which he promptly refused – Fina knocked on the door.

"Come in!" she heard a muffled voice say.

Opening the door revealed a surprisingly spacious cabin, filled, but not overstuffed, with furniture and paintings. Two comfy looking beds occupied most of the room, but the corner held a mahogany wardrobe and writing desk. A sandstone statue of a parrot stood watch balefully over the stationery supplies on the desk. Above the desk hung a red and orange painting of a sunset, bringing an extra warmth – not heat, thank goodness – to the room. Turning around, she saw a tiny turtle, carved out of wood, perched on a ledge above the door. She smiled to herself, thinking it a welcome talisman for the voyage.

The open suitcase filled with neatly folded squares on one counterpane indicated Ruby had already selected her bed. Ruby exited the bathroom at that moment and collapsed onto the bed. Her shoulders were hunched, and she grasped her favourite blue handkerchief – a gift from her late grandmother in St Kitts – tightly in her hand, as if it might wriggle out and escape at any moment.

Fina thought the look on her own face must have betrayed her feelings about Ruby's abrupt exit. Ruby nodded her head, as if to agree with her own unspoken words.

"I apologise for just leaving you behind like that," said Ruby. "I was so taken aback by what I surmised was Ian's apparition that I promptly forgot all of my manners." She dabbed her forehead lightly with the handkerchief.

"It is surprising, but I cannot understand why you wouldn't be pleased to see him. After all, you two were so close at Pauncefort..." said Fina, collapsing on her bed and staring up at the ceiling.

"Yes, well, I'm happy to see him for just that reason. But I couldn't help but think that the coincidence is a little too convenient. After all, he had plenty of opportunities to call on me in Oxford after the ghastly business at Pauncefort. And he didn't. And now he just happens to be on the same ship?" she said, shaking her head.

"So if he's not here for romantic reasons, do you think he's following us because of our, ah, other activities?" enquired Fina, suddenly sitting up. "After all, we did reveal to him our association with anti-colonial campaigns when we were at Pauncefort. But are we really important enough to follow all the way here?"

Ruby's upper body rocked to and fro in agreement. "It is hard to believe that two young women pose a threat, but remember who we are. Police always pay attention to me, no matter how much I dress up. I also have family in the Caribbean, some of whom I suspect are being watched by local authorities. And you..."

"Yes, I suppose if they found out about my Irish side of the family – not to mention my political sympathies."

"And your family's case," whispered Ruby. As soon as she uttered those words, she looked horrified by her misstep.

Fina's mind froze. Her brother's face. Connor. His look of anguish as the judge pronounced him guilty of her father's murder.

Ruby sat quietly for a moment. Then she began again. She had clearly learned how to respond to Fina in such a way that she brought her friend back to reality – freeing her, at least temporarily, from those painful memories.

"Even if we weren't important enough to spy on, I've heard whisperings that Ian's theatre producer career might not be as genuine as it seems," said Ruby, quietly. "I'm not so much upset that we have someone spying on us, but rather that it is he – and the implications of it. He must be working for the British government, a business, or some British government agency in the Bahamas."

"No!" said Fina, firmly. "I simply cannot believe it. You know I am a good judge of character—"

"One of the many reasons why I appreciate you so much, dear friend," interjected Ruby with a flicker of a smile.

Fina returned the grin and continued. "And I think Ian is a good one to his core. I cannot believe he'd spy on us."

"I agree with you, but it may be that Ian was forced into doing it," said Ruby. "We've known of cases where the British government forces good people to work for them, threatening them or their families if they do not. What makes it worse is that we actually *are* on a mission this time."

3
____

Fina lifted herself halfway off the bed to look Ruby in the eye. "What exactly *is* our mission?" Ruby didn't answer. She stared at the curtains, even though they were pulled closed.

"Ruby?"

Her eyes darted quickly from side to side, as if she were waking up. "Sorry. I'm still thinking about – or I should say worrying – about Ian."

"How about this? Let's not jump to conclusions about Ian – but we will be sufficiently wary. Agreed? You know I say that as your friend."

Nodding in agreement, Ruby pulled a crisp blue envelope out of her handbag with a flourish. She slid it toward Fina on the bed.

"I present you with our mission. A letter from my brother."

Fina scrutinised the envelope. The postmark read St Kitts. She was looking forward to meeting Ruby's brother again after their first encounter in Oxford. On their return trip from Trinidad, Ruby and Fina were planning a short stop in St Kitts to see Ruby's family.

Glancing at the letter, however, Fina raised her eyebrow. It was addressed to a "Miss Emerald Byrdcroft". Must be Ruby's code name. She opened the envelope, fell back onto the cool counterpane, and began to read.

Dear Emerald:

I write you aboard the SS Sanguine, bound for Port of Spain. Thus far, I have had an uneventful journey. It took me the first day to adjust to the rocking and bobbing of the ship. Once I emerged from my lair, however, I felt much revived. The crew have been delightful. The food has been unexpectedly delicious and the company only slightly less so. The twelve passengers, counting myself, get on reasonably well. You know how it is – a ship brings people together quite quickly. They confess secrets that they'd never even tell their closest friends. Or family. Of course, I haven't solicited these secrets, but they've been forthcoming nonetheless. Most of these secrets have been from white Britishers, who feel that my role must be one of confidant. I play up to them, mostly out of amusement but also because I'm genuinely interested. There is one person in particular who interests me.

But enough of my ramblings. I trust you are well and that you'll write me with any news you have forthwith.

With love and affection,

Delwyn

Fina stuffed the letter back into its envelope and sat up with a sudden movement. "Clever code names," she smiled. "What does it all mean?" She giggled. "I'm at sea!"

"Quite funny, Feens. Sometimes I think Wendell is too clever for his own good. All I know is that the letter is supposed to indicate by whom and when we'll be contacted."

"Contacted for what? I've been waiting for you to tell me since we sailed from Southampton!"

"You know about the labour unrest that's building across the Caribbean. It's at a fever pitch in Trinidad and Tobago right now, which is partially why I leaped at the chance to go with Gustave to Port of Spain. Our organisation has certain information about three owners of very large companies that are the most abusive to workers."

"What kind of information – or can't you tell me what it is?"

"What I know I can tell you. The information is about illegal financial activities. If local governments were to find out, they'd have to do something. The idea is that this would temporarily give the workers' movements some leverage, or at least more time to mobilise."

Ruby took a long sip of water and continued. "We are supposed to be contacted by someone on this ship. You know this is an international organisation, so nationality won't help us narrow anything down this time. They are supposed to impart a message, item or something – I don't know what – to us, which I am to deliver to a contact in Port of Spain. I do not know exactly what it is about, or the identity of the person who will deliver it."

"Do you know the contact in Port of Spain?" asked Fina.

"I don't know that either. I suppose that information will be entrusted to us when this person gets in touch with us aboard the ship."

"Crikey. Wendell must think we're awfully clever."

Ruby leaned back on her bed. "Sometimes I think this is his way of getting revenge for me being the older sibling. When we were little I could be rather, well, strict with him."

"Never! Not you," said Fina, throwing a small bed pillow at Ruby in jest.

There was a knock at the door.

Fina opened the door to a compact, neat man whose eyes bulged. It seemed to be a permanent rather than a temporary state, thought Fina. He wore a maroon suit, which elevated his rather obviously quiet personality. His cropped, tidy hair framed a baby face, though Fina guessed he must be in his late forties. He took a long drag on a tiny black cigarette.

"I'm Gustave Marchand, here to see Miss Dove," he said,

holding out his hand. Fina took it and shook it rather perfunctorily. This was not how she had pictured the famous new designer. The maroon suit, yes, but not the rest of the man.

"Pleased to meet you, Mr Marchand. Do come in. I'm Fina Aubrey-Havelock. I'm so grateful to you for helping to arrange for my passage to Trinidad. The two of us were just chatting and unpacking," said Fina, striding toward her suitcase as if to prove that was indeed what she had been doing.

"A pleasure to meet you, Miss Aubrey-Havelock. So glad you could join us."

Fina's throat closed and her chest tightened. Here it came: the inevitable inquisitive reaction to the announcement of her last name. But Gustave Marchand remained impassive, devoid of curiosity. No questions about her father's murder were forthcoming.

She was powerless to stop the flood of memories again. For months, the townsfolk back in Tavistock had whispered behind her back, and sometimes to her face, about Connor. Most of them believed her brother had murdered their father – a crime for which he had been hanged. Those were the people she could still not look in the eye.

This time, however, as she watched Marchand cast an assessing eye over the clothes laid out on the bed, she noticed a little twinge in her stomach. It was the kind of twinge she experienced when she had doubt. Doubt about what?

Perhaps he hadn't heard about the case in Paris – although that was hard to believe, given the relentless newspaper coverage, thought Fina. In any case, it was a relief. She let out a little puff of air that ruffled the fringe on her forehead. Maybe was just being kind.

Ruby smoothed her hair and dress and arose from her reclined position on the bed. She directed Gustave toward a chair in the corner. He waved it away. "Ruby, my dear, exciting news. I've come to inform you that Dolores Dominguez is on our voyage!" He practically squeaked these words, though his face remained stony. It was as if his words had been spoken by a ventriloquist.

"What?!" exclaimed Ruby. "But I adore her. I'll never forget her in *Blue Hyacinths*."

Gustave's lips, still frozen along with the rest of his facial muscles, said, "I know, dear Ruby. Her cabin is located next to mine, and we've just had a marvellous chat about her films. We also talked about my clothes. She is looking for some new designs, so we have a grand opportunity. Come – let us discuss!"

Ruby positively glowed. She looked at Fina.

"Please, please, Ruby. Do go on! I must find Victor soon, in any case. We will have a whole five days to talk before we reach Port of Spain."

And with that, Ruby scooped up her scarlet clutch and floated out of the room.

Thud. Thud.

Fina squinted at the ceiling fixture, which had begun to swing, to and fro, like a child on a swing.

4

———

"Fi-na, Fi-na, Fi-na!" came the muffled cadence from the adjoining cabin.

Must be dear Victor, she thought. The pounding stopped, but she had her summons. Sighing at her as-yet-unpacked suitcase, she locked the cabin and made her way to the adjoining cabin. Sadie opened the door.

The room, a mirror image of her own, looked as if a small band of sprites had sprung open bags of clothes and toys at strategic intervals throughout the room. Gauzy crimson and tangerine scarves had escaped the confines of luggage, adorning a picture here and a chair there. Overlooking it all were a carved wooden turtle and a sandstone parrot, twins to the ones in her own cabin.

Sadie nestled into a small armchair, apparently unperturbed by this state of affairs. One of her crossed legs swung languidly. She sipped from a glass with beads of condensation from the clash of hot air and cold liquid. Fina cast a jealous eye over her sea green voile dressing gown.

Victor glanced up from the small wooden horse he was

holding in intense concentration. He bounded over to Fina. "Fi-na! Fi-na! Can we play now?"

His mother, ignoring Victor's enquiry, said, "Dear Fina. I apologise for the awful racket. Victor began pounding while I was getting ready for the bath."

"No trouble at all, Sadie. How often would you like me to see after Victor? Or perhaps a better question is how much time would you like me to spend on lessons?"

"Lessons..." said Sadie vaguely. "The thing is, I don't want Victor picking up my American accent and all of my American-isms. I want him to grow up to be a real English gentleman," she said, waving her hands enthusiastically.

Fina groaned inwardly. So-called real English gentlemen were the scourge of her world.

As if on cue, Victor squeaked, "Stick 'em up, you broad!"

"Victor!" squealed his mother, craning her neck in the direction of her son. "Behave yourself. Otherwise Fina will make you stay inside learning proper English pronunciation for the whole trip. You wouldn't want that, would you?"

Victor's little eyebrows shot up in horror. "Yes, I mean no, Mama."

"You really should call me 'mummy' or 'mother', Victor. 'Mama' isn't proper."

Sadie twisted her neck back toward Fina. "I think three hours a day for elocution should be enough. And if you can watch over him, as needed – I'll let you know. Otherwise you're free to do as you please."

She took a compact from the side table and began to powder her nose.

"That's splendid, Sadie. Thank you," said Fina. "There seems to be another younger boy on board – is it all right if they play together?" Her request was more tentative than she would have liked, but she feared there was every chance Sadie would object.

After all, from what she had seen, that family was hardly in the same class as the family of the late Lord Winchcombe-Twisleton.

Sadie, however, didn't bother to put down her compact. "Oh, I suppose so," she said airily. "The little English boy, with those darling flannel shorts? As long as they stay out of trouble."

Fina crouched down on the floor to talk to Victor, moving a herd of toy horses out of the way.

"Come along, Victor. I'm sure your mother wants to unpack more," Fina said before she could stop herself. The implication was that she must want to tidy up the room since it was obvious that the suitcases had already unpacked themselves.

If Sadie were offended, she didn't show it. Fina suspected that underneath all that silk and gloss lurked a woman of granite.

"Actually, all I crave right now is a lukewarm bath after this terrible heat," Sadie said, gently flapping the passenger manifest in front of her face. She rose and plucked another dressing gown – this time in chartreuse silk – from the bedpost. Then she sauntered into the bathroom.

Preparing to explore the ship, Fina hunted about for a few children's books, in case they found a cosy place to read. As she lifted them up from the bed, a slip of paper fluttered to the floor. She glanced at the bathroom door. It was shut. She could hear bathwater running and gentle humming.

Victor snuffled as his toy hedgehog ambled across the carpet.

Fina couldn't help herself. She unfolded the paper.

Though it was written on letter paper, it contained only two rather spidery lines without a salutation or closing: "flour 20 grams, potatoes 20 grams, rice 20 grams".

Must be a note about a slimming regime, thought Fina. Sadie was thin as a wafer. Fina grudgingly admired her own curves in the mirror fastened to the door. Or could it be some sort of code?

She turned to Victor, who was engrossed in playing with a giraffe which had seen better days. He made small meowing noises which Fina heard as the cries of the giraffe to be left in peace.

"Victor, are you prepared to explore the ship? I certainly am. Perhaps we can find something to nibble on while we're out and about."

Victor stood up and removed a small rectangular object encased in shiny wrapping from his pocket. He proffered it to Fina like it was a special discovery. "You can share my Mars bar," he said, proudly. "It's scrumptious."

Fina peered at the crumpled wrapper, smeared with chocolate on the outside. She suspected it had been melted and reformed at least a dozen times. Not wanting to hurt his feelings, she said, "My, that is generous of you. I will take it and put it in my bag for later." She took the item and carefully wrapped it in a handkerchief and then slipped it into her bag.

Offering her hand, she said, "I saw another child on the ship – let's find him!" Hand in hand, they set off on their adventure.

5

———

"Mooooo." The ship's mournful horn sounded. A moment later, a great jolt nearly catapulted Victor through the railing onto the lower deck. Fina grabbed his shirt before he slid off into oblivion.

"Whoa!" he yelled with delight. "That was fun."

Never wanting to miss a good moment for a lesson, Fina gasped, "You could say, 'That was delightful!' or 'Smashing!'." He grinned up at her and scampered down the deck toward the bow of the ship.

As she caught up with him, she held out the passenger manifest and map of the boat. "Let's play a game, Victor. I have the map of the ship here. I wonder how many rooms you can identify by what is inside. I'll tell you your options and you try to guess."

"Right-o. Here is the first room!"

After they passed cabin 3 – Fina noted this belonged to a Patricia Burbage and Emeline Caulk – they turned left into a half-octagonal room encased with floor-to-ceiling windows.

A wall of scent assaulted Fina's olfactory glands as they entered. Even though she had always been sensitive to odours, this peculiarity always surprised her when it happened. The heavy, earthy scent of roses would be pleasant if it were a bit subtler.

Gripping the door handle, she collapsed into an overstuffed chair near an open window at the front. She gulped the salty breeze. A newspaper lay on the side table, and she picked it up, desperate for a distraction. It was dated 3rd May 1935. Three weeks old! Well, it was better than nothing. Feeling less queasy, she watched Victor skip in little circles round the room.

"Victor!" she hissed, waving him over to the chair. "Come here! Don't disturb those guests."

Victor complied, bouncing over to an adjacent chair. He wiggled himself up onto the seat – and then continued to wiggle.

"Jolly ship!" he said, thumping his arms on the chair as if he were a man of more advanced years. He leaned in toward Fina. "Those people in the corner are whispering."

Fina nodded and surreptitiously glanced at the two passengers ensconced in high-back chairs across from one another. One of them must be the source of the perfume. The first one wore a simple yet expensively tailored blue linen frock. The boat-neck line revealed a graceful neck and shoulders, interrupted only by long glass bead earrings. Her body was bent a hairbreadth's distance toward the other figure, clad in an orange linen shirt and white trousers. His rather long but exquisitely coiffed hair just brushed the jawline of his chiselled face.

Realising that she was staring, she purposely turned to Victor. "So what room do you think this is, young Victor? I'll tell you your choices: the reading room, the kitchen—"

"Ha, this isn't the kitchen!" he said in a fit of giggles.

"The kitchen," she repeated with a grin, "the dining room, the lounge, the bar, the green room or the crew's quarters?"

"Hmm," he said, while his little head scanned the room like

a searchlight. Despite the perfume, the room had a calming effect on Fina. It was lined with shelves on the far wall holding various knick-knacks, and colourful chairs and tables were scattered about the room.

"Is it the reading room?" enquired Victor.

"Why do you say that?"

"There are some books on that far wall."

"Excellent guess, but this is the lounge, not the reading room. Let's move on to our next station," said Fina promptly rising from the chair. The pair weaved in and out of the tables and chairs to exit through the far door. Fina endeavoured to look nonchalant as they passed the two conversationalists.

She and Victor could have been two ghostly apparitions floating by, unnoticed.

"Dolores, you know this will all die down soon," the man growled. "Journalists have their moment, but they soon grow bored if the story is too hard to cover." He cupped his hand over hers. Was it a libidinous, paternalistic or genuinely caring gesture? The tension between the pair clashed awkwardly with the comfortable furnishings of the cosy room.

"I hope so. Perhaps the next few months away will prove you right, Balraj," she sighed, leaving her hand in place.

This must be the famous Dolores Dominguez, the film star, thought Fina. She didn't recognise her, but why should she – she hadn't seen her in the cinema. Fina always expected that famous people would be instantly recognisable, just because they were famous.

Crash!

As Victor toddled out of the lounge, he bumped into a woman wearing a maid's uniform. A tea set and tray had clattered to the floor.

"Victor!" scolded Fina, feeling her body suddenly become a conduit for her own mother's voice. "Please mind your step!"

Victor hung his head in shame.

"That's all right, young master Victor," said the woman. She bent over to help Fina gather up the detritus on the deck. "These things happen at close quarters, especially when the ship gets to rocking in stormy weather!" she said with a short laugh, almost a hiccough.

As the puddle of cooling tea spread across the floorboards, Fina snatched quickly at an endangered paper napkin. Half the napkin was covered with a meticulously sketched ink portrait. An amazing resemblance to the man she had just seen inside the lounge. The pen strokes were quick yet sure, obviously the result of much practise.

As she stood up to give back the tray, Fina said, "I'm Fina Aubrey-Havelock," holding out her hand.

The maid wiped her hands on her apron and returned the gesture. "Agnes is the name, Agnes Gidge, Miss Aubrey-Havelock. Pleased to meet you and young master Victor here. I'll be seeing to your rooms while on board."

Fina peered at Agnes. The stout and doughy woman's face was covered in make-up. It was skilfully applied, but it was so unusual that Fina gawped at her. She noticed that the maid's cap was set at an unusually rakish angle.

Putting two and two together, Fina said, "I noticed that drawing on the paper napkin I picked up with the tray. It was marvellous – was it your drawing?"

Agnes' orangish skin flushed with pleasure. "Yes, miss. I cannot help myself. Loved to doodle since I was a small child. Sarah – she's the cook and she's a poet! I don't even like poetry myself, but I like her little rhymes. Why, just the other day, she wrote one about one of the stewards, Lev. She even wrote one about the captain," Agnes prattled on.

To halt the stream of words, Fina said, "My, my, quite a

number of artists on board. Dolores Dominguez. And Balraj Chadha!" She pointed to the portrait.

Beaming with pleasure, Agnes said, "Oh yes, miss. The actor. Ever so handsome, isn't he? Mind you, he has quite an eye for the ladies. You'd better watch yourself around him. Now, who else was saying the same thing to me just this morning?"

Fina was distracted suddenly by the silence. The silence of Victor.

"So sorry, Miss Gidge. It seems I've lost Victor. Must dash."

6

Running – actually sliding – down the shiny pinewood flooring, Fina leaned in to the left as she came to the end of the deck. Though she was worried about Victor, she was rather enjoying the feeling of ice skating on deck.

With a throbbing heart and pounding head, she peered around a row of chairs. Victor might be playing a game of sardines.

Hearing gentle peals of laughter, she swivelled round and stepped into what must be the reading room. Victor swung his legs from a high chair, munching greedily on a banana. Fina let out a great whoosh of air.

Next to Victor sat a man in a white uniform, more formal than the one she had seen on Lev. While Lev had an anxious, hunted look on his face, this man looked perfectly at ease. One arm was draped over the chair, while the other held the stub of a lit cigarette.

"Victor!" she heard herself cry – there was her mother again. "You gave me such a fright! Please do not run off like that again."

"No harm done, miss, as we're on a ship," said the man, blowing a smoke ring away from Victor and Fina.

Heat crept up Fina's neck, like a tiny procession of pinpricks marching toward her face. "As you say, we're on a ship. That is precisely why I should worry. Why, Victor nearly flew overboard when the ship lurched earlier."

"Ah, miss, that's just him getting used to his sea legs."

"His, his what?" Fina knew she was as red as a beetroot by now in full-blown indignation. Really. The nerve.

"S-e-a l-e-g-s, miss," he said in slow tones.

"I know what sea legs are, sir. My brother—" She stopped. The room shifted and began to spin. Fortunately, a chair caught her before she tumbled to the floor.

As her eyes shut, an image rose before her of her brother in the boat, laughing. Could it really only be two years ago? Behind him was her father, who gave a great snort of laughter in return. The cold wind gusted spray from the Channel into their faces.

"You look as though you still need to find your sea legs yourself, miss."

Opening her eyes, Fina stared at the man again. Those eyes hold no malice, she thought. Blast it, he was infuriating.

"No, no. I just remembered something. I'm thirsty and rather ravenous," she said.

The man leaned behind his chair and scooped up a tray, laden with iced tea and bananas. Without a word, she took the tray and began to make quick work of its contents.

The refreshing iced tea slid down her throat. The sweet, sticky starchiness of the banana immediately began to quell her queasiness. More at ease now, she absorbed the energy of her surroundings. The reading room reminded her of home – books everywhere and comfortable chairs in which to read them.

As she scanned the room, she saw out of the corner of her eye that the man held his gaze on her. "I'd better introduce myself," he said. "I'm Neville Emmanuel Raymond, lead steward on the ship. Born and bred in the Bahamas."

Fina returned the gaze. "Pleased to meet you, Mr Raymond. I'm Fina Aubrey-Havelock, temporary governess to young Victor here. Thank you for taking care of him," she said, stopping herself before she began to apologise to him for her testiness earlier. After all, the man had been rather impertinent in his assumptions. "And thank you for the tea and bananas. I simply adore bananas."

"So does young Victor here – I believe he's starting his fourth go-round," said Neville with a gleam of mischief in his eyes.

"Good gracious! You will have quite the bellyache," she said as she saw Victor chomping down rhythmically. His eyelids fell to half mast, jerking up again, and then slowly slid down. He must be exhausted. Quickly turning from Victor to Neville, she was astonished to see that he had been staring at her again. Feeling a mixture of shame and discomfort, she rose to peruse the books on the shelves.

As she ran her finger along the book spines, Neville said, "Can I help you find something?"

"I devour mysteries, preferably ones of the locked room sort. But I also enjoy reading politics," she said.

Neville rocketed out of his seat. His relaxed and somewhat self-satisfied manner had vanished. "Well, now. Ah, if you're seeking a ripping mystery, try Ngaio Marsh's *A Man Lay Dead*," he said, offering her a small red, leather-bound volume.

Fina nodded her head. She had read this book a few times already, but she didn't want to disappoint him. Besides, it had been at least a year since she last read it. They had five days of rest and relative relaxation before the excitement waiting in Port of Spain. She would have plenty of time to revisit this comforting book.

"And for politics?"

Neville waved his arms to and fro across the bookshelves,

scanning them carefully. He came to an abrupt halt as his finger touched a small brown volume.

"Here you are. Lev recommended it – a collection of Nestor Makhno's essays. I am curious to see if you will find it... too provocative," he said, drawing out the last word. Really, the man was quite cheeky, she thought.

"Thank you, Mr Raymond," she said accepting her gifts without responding to Mr Raymond's own provocation. "Victor and I must be on our way."

But Victor lay slumped in the chair, cradling his fourth banana peel like a baby. Neville gathered up the narcoleptic child and gently whisked him out of the room.

Nestor Makhno, she repeated in her head. It was rather provocative – downright dangerous to some – to offer a passenger the essays of a Ukrainian anarchist.

7

Nothing. Back in her cabin, Fina shook the Makhno volume, willing it to give up its secrets. No slips of paper fluttered to the ground. No discreetly pasted-together pages, no secret folders, and no tellingly underlined words or notes in the volume. Selkies and kelpies. It must mean something, she thought. Why else would a steward give an unknown guest an anarchist book?

Perhaps he was their contact? It seemed too easy, she thought as she threw the book on the bed in frustration.

The sugar of the banana and caffeine of the iced tea fuelled a sudden burst of energy. She busied herself with the neglected task of unpacking – a pleasure in life she had in common with Ruby. Perhaps that was one of the reasons they were good friends. She pulled out a flowery chiffon frock with flutter sleeves and draped it over the bed. It was her one small – well, rather large, really – splurge she had made for this trip. It wasn't her style, but she had decided it was a good time to branch out a bit.

As she stepped into the bathroom to arrange her toiletries, she heard a key turn in the lock.

Ruby stumbled into the room. The performance was reminiscent of a drunken sailor, though Fina had never witnessed this clichéd spectacle herself.

Fina rushed over and steadied her friend. "Here, come sit down on your bed." She peered more closely at her friend. Beads of sweat lined her forehead. Ruby never sweated – at least not visibly. That was Fina's department.

"What is the matter?"

Ruby collapsed back on the bed, clutching her stomach. "I am so queasy and feverish. Do you think I'm ill?

"Do you feel weak?" asked Fina.

"No."

"I wouldn't wonder if it were a combination of the heat and seasickness."

"Perhaps," said Ruby, rather grudgingly. "But maybe it's just something I ate?"

"Here," said Fina, going to the pitcher on the bedside table to fill a glass of water. "Drink this. I think I have some pills that might help, but they're not designed for seasickness, exactly."

As she rummaged in her sponge bag, Fina recounted her adventures thus far. Ruby swallowed the pills with great effort and then collapsed again on the bed. "I feel awful, Feens, but we can still talk. What you say about Neville is definitely intriguing. Hmm. He definitely seems to have piqued your curiosity," she said, giving Fina a half-hearted wink, though it was a wink nonetheless. "I wish I could read that Makhno book myself, but I do think it will only make me more ill right now."

"Of course," said Fina. "You should rest." She lay back on the bed, and then sat up with a jerk. "I forgot to mention that I saw Dolores Dominguez!"

After Fina recounted the conversation she had overheard, Ruby grew so excited that she lifted herself up on her elbows. "Gustave and I met her and she asked to see some of my sketches. It is a great opportunity for me. I really admire her so much, especially because she 'made it big' as the Americans say – in Hollywood. Can you imagine if she wore some of my designs in a film?"

Despite her obvious and somewhat uncharacteristic gushing enthusiasm, Ruby's elbows gave way and she sank back into the sheets. Fina gave Ruby a wan smile of knowing appreciation.

Ominous gurgling noises could be heard coming from Fina's stomach, despite her snack. She peered at the clock on the opposite wall. 4:50. "Drinks are at 5:30. Perhaps you should rest here. I'll go and report back to you about what I learn."

"I, ah, oh yes, I suppose you're right," said Ruby with great effort. Patting her friend on the hand, Fina gathered her chiffon dress, sponge bag and handbag and whisked into the bathroom. Leaving the door open ajar, she said rather loudly, "Shall we continue to talk while I dress?"

"Yes, though there's no need to shout, dear one. My illness hasn't stolen my hearing."

Touchy, thought Fina. Must be that she's not feeling well.

"Sorry. So what else did you learn on your adventure this afternoon," Fina said, slipping off her day dress and sliding into the chiffon.

"I forgot to tell you one thing. It's not really important to our mission – but I did want to alert you about some rather unpleasant fellow passengers. What were their names? One was rather tall in tweed and the other was shorter – but still quite tall – in silk. Not only were they rude, but the tall one made some comment about my colour that I'd rather not repeat."

"I wonder if that's the same pair that nearly knocked me overboard with their suitcase? Wait." Fina withdrew the passenger manifest from her handbag. "The only two women travelling together are Miss Emeline Caulk and Mrs Patricia Burbage."

"That's it!" yelled Ruby, though she was so weak it sounded

more like a protesting whimper. "The one in the tweed referred to the other one as Patricia. Patricia also seems to have a wandering eye, dear one, so watch yourself. I already noticed the way she looked at me."

"Don't worry," giggled Fina, her lipstick application now resembling a circus clown's lips. "She's not my type. Too serious."

"Ta-da!" she continued, sweeping out of the bathroom. "What do you think?"

"Fabulous Fina, as always," said Ruby with a weak smile.

Sighing with pleasure, Fina sat on the edge of the bed. "Now, what shall I do at drinks? Look for someone in particular? Some furtive sign? Should I give a sign?"

"Well, other than keeping an eye on Ian and..."

Fina shook her head in disapprobation.

"I know, I know what you said about him," Ruby responded. "Just don't get too cosy with him, especially if there's drinks. I'm worried that you might spill the so-called beans."

"What? Me?" said Fina, sticking out her lower lip.

"You know this isn't about you, Feens. I didn't mean to say anything about you, personally – it's just the situation. It could happen easily to anyone, especially if they don't have a friend there to pull them away at the right moment."

"I suppose you're right. You were about to say something else, though – about keeping an eye on..."

"Ah, sorry. I'm having trouble focusing. Just be your charming self and gather juicy details about our companions."

A slithering noise came from underneath the cabin door.

Fina rose. Perhaps someone was preparing to knock. Instead, she saw a small envelope, addressed to Ruby, had been slid under the door.

"It's a letter for you," she reported, handing the missive to Ruby.

"Ugh," groaned Ruby, pushing it away and turning on her side. "Just the thought of reading it turns my stomach. Would you read it?"

"It says: 'Dearest Ruby, Please meet me in the reading room at midnight. Yours ever, Ian.'

Ooh! A lovers' tryst!"

"Hardly. I think he feels guilty about sneaking up on us like this. I'm afraid you'll have to tell him I am ill – which is true. And now, dear one, I have to sleep," said Ruby, pulling the covers over her head.

The familiar butterfly of social anxiety began to flutter in her stomach. Determined to ignore it, Fina placed her clutch firmly underneath her arm and marched out to meet her destiny – or at least to find a fine beverage to calm her jangled nerves.

8

A cool breeze wafted over her as she stepped out of the cabin. Fina had a sudden brainwave. What better way to avoid her anxiety? She'd make an entrance with Sadie and Victor. Feeling quite satisfied with herself, she tapped on the door. Sadie flung the door open so quickly it was as if she had been eagerly awaiting her arrival.

"Oh," she said, her smile quickly disappearing. "It's you."

"Were you expecting someone else?" asked Fina.

Ignoring her question, Sadie replied, "I'm so sorry, Fina. It is delightful to see you. We were just about to depart. Won't you join us?"

Fina had predicted her employer's style correctly: slinky. Sadie sauntered out of the cabin in an ankle-length raspberry number, form-fitting but hardly snug. The dramatic open back contrasted with the rather demure cowl neck in the front. A bevy of bangles clicked pleasantly when she reached up to fluff her impossibly blonde hair.

Victor was clad in a ridiculously adorable linen blazer affair with short pants and a tie that resembled a faux black gardenia. The tie appeared to be nearly choking him, but he was completely oblivious – too engrossed by a soft pink plasticine rabbit. He made little grunting noises while twitching his nose, apparently expecting a return gesture from the rabbit.

"That would be spiffing!" gushed Fina with relief. And with that, they trundled down the deck to the stairs leading to the second floor of the ship. Fina knew from her careful study of the map earlier that there were four decks. The lower deck housed the crew, minus the captain. The first deck held the passenger cabins, plus the lounge and reading room. The second held the kitchen, dining room, captain's quarters plus bedroom, as well as the green room. The top deck – where they were headed now – held a sun deck with a quoits pitch, a bar and the bridge.

Squinting at the direct sun, Fina shielded her eyes to survey the scene at the bar. By her estimation, most of the guests had arrived. The bar itself was simply that – a long, wooden, closed-in table with a variety of spirits held in beautiful bottles, next to a few already-prepared cool green and blue cocktails. Lev stood behind the bar in intense concentration, mixing drinks. Fina thought he might start juggling the two shakers.

A few scattered tables and lounge chairs dotted the deck around the bar. Dolores Dominguez lay in one of the lounge chairs, fanning herself with the passenger manifest. She held a cigarette loosely in the other hand. When the ash threatened to fall on the deck, she made a liquid movement to ensure it found its resting place in the ashtray by her side. She looked divine in a simple navy gown which would have looked plain on someone else. Even if Fina hadn't known Dolores was a film star, she would have still thought her devastatingly glamourous.

Dolores appeared perfectly at home by herself – neither bored nor overly excited, surveying the room as if it were her own party.

Two lounge chairs over from Dolores reclined the woman in the flowered frock Fina had seen earlier, the mother of the five-year-old. After studying the passenger list closely, Fina determined this must be Violet Gibbs. Unlike Dolores, Violet was shrinking and wilting, thought Fina. She mentally took herself to task for her inward joke in poor taste. Really, why was the woman at the bar at all? She looked just as vaguely ill as she had a few hours ago upon their embarkation on the SS *Sanguine*. Certainly she wasn't happy to relax in her recliner. She looked like a patient in a dentist's chair: uncomfortable and vulnerable.

Violet's husband, Phillip, and her son, Gilbert, sat next to her. The family was a study in contrasts, thought Fina. Phillip, still in his shabby brown suit but surprisingly sharp toe-cap Oxfords, was enjoying his blue cocktail. His leg jiggled up and down as he took tiny sips from the glass. Gilbert blew bubbles with a little wand. He seemed to be trying to irritate his mother by blowing them in her direction. And succeeding, as Fina could see by the expression on her face.

A hand gently grazed Fina's arm. Twirling around, she faced the comfortable dumpling figure of Gustave Marchand.

"Darling – I may call you Fina?" he said. There again was that odd mismatch of a beautiful, enthusiastic voice with a rather inelastic, stony face.

Setting her cocktail glass down on a nearby table after she had sloshed a bit on her gown – why are you so clumsy, she thought to herself – she shook his hand.

"Of course, Mr Marchand. May I call you Gustave?"

"Please do, my dear lady, of course, of course. I see you are a keen observer of other human beings. It is a little hobby of my own, you see. I always recognise a – how do you say? Kindred spirit."

Though the alcohol had smoothed over some of the edges of Fina's anxiety – both that normal social anxiety as well as the additional pressure to gather information – this question prompted her heart to palpitate. Had he been watching her?

The arrival of Emeline Caulk and Patricia Burbage rescued Fina from answering Gustave's awkward comment. Patricia was certainly elegant. She shone in a long, flowing, royal purple crepe gown. A powder blue chiffon scarf, artfully arranged at her neck, was pinned into place by a positively enormous starfish brooch. The little spines and bumps on the silver starfish sparkled. They couldn't be real – not that many diamonds, surely? She scanned her passenger manifest as if it would hold the answer.

Gustave leaned over. He whispered, "Yes, darling, I wouldn't be surprised if those were diamonds. She isn't one to hide her millions. Do you see the size of that pearl ring?"

Fina had never seen a pearl that large in her life. Though the overall effect of the ring and brooch could have been overwhelming or vulgar – though Fina strongly suspected she didn't like the implications of that word – Patricia's bearing somehow counteracted the heaviness of her jewels. She looked oddly defiant, as though she had had to nerve herself to enter the arena. Yet no one here was remotely threatening.

Emeline, still clad in stiff tweeds, sat down on the edge of a lounge chair. As Patricia swept over to the bar, she turned her head and stared at Sadie. And Sadie stared back. Definitely intriguing.

Though it could just be the champagne, Fina thought Gustave could be a confidant of sorts. She whispered back, "Who is she, really? Was she born into wealth?"

"She married into her wealth," he sighed wistfully. "Henry Burbage. The Canadian. Surely you must have heard of Burbage Oil?"

"That's it!" said Fina, adding, "I mean, I knew something was familiar about her name." In her excitement, Fina had sprayed a little more of her drink, though fortunately not on Gustave. He still brushed his jacket, absently.

"But where is her husband? Are they estranged? And what do you know about Emeline?" enquired Fina.

"Her husband died – I believe it was a little over a year ago. A tragic accident involving a donkey. That left her the majority shareholder in his company. So Mrs Burbage is, as the Americans say, rolling in it."

"Oh dear," said Fina, hoping he would expand on the theme of the donkey.

Instead, he expanded on her second question. "Emeline Caulk is Patricia's sister," he said, puckering his mouth when he said "sister". It was the first time Fina had seen his facial muscles engage in any physical activity.

"Do you mean she's not really her sister?"

"No, no. I mean, dear lady, that I cannot believe the two are actually related to one another. Miss Caulk is, well, I do not wish to be unkind, but as a designer, I must say..."

"Could use better clothes?" Fina said, rescuing him.

"Well, yes, though I suspect they would not fit her well. She is rather, well, stiff. She has energy and vitality, but that rigidity! I feel sorry for her."

Fina was at a loss for words in response to Gustave's comment, so she took another sip of her rapidly vanishing cocktail. She excused herself and traipsed to the bar. Out of the corner of her eye, she saw the man she knew to be Balraj. Even from her vantage point, she could see he was going to make, as they say in the theatre, "an entrance".

"Darling, darling, darling Sadie... or is it Lady Whatsit?" he called out to Sadie, as if the other passengers were merely furniture. Sadie plopped down in a nearby chair with sudden force. If the chair hadn't been there, Fina was sure she would have fallen onto the deck.

She peered again at her passenger list. Balraj Chadha was listed, quite clearly. How could Sadie have failed to notice his name? Fina's anxious mind could not comprehend how anyone could forgo reading the passenger list most carefully.

Balraj was clad in azure from head to toe. He glided across the deck like a great wave seeking a shoreline.

"It's Lady Winchcombe-Twisleton, as you well know, Mr Chadha," said Sadie, her back rigid. She rose from her chair and gripped the railing.

As Balraj leaned over to peck Sadie's cheek, she ducked, nearly sending him toppling over. He regained his footing immediately and brushed his hair out of his eyes.

"Why so formal, *Lady* Twislecombe-Winchton?" Fina felt sure he had mangled her name on purpose.

None of the other passengers had moved during this display – they were all focused intently on the unfolding drama.

Sadie marched past Balraj toward the corner where Victor and his new friend, Gilbert, were making crashing noises with their toys. She almost yanked Victor's arm out of his socket in her hurry to make an exit. Half dragging him across the floor to the nearest staircase, she descended below without a word – except for Victor's faint protests.

Fina was still at the bar, staring. Lev shook his head while pouring another drink.

"Rich people," he muttered under his breath. Surely he knew Fina could hear him. Did he not care?

"I wonder what that was about," said Fina, eyeing Lev speculatively. Her eyes slid over to the moist red fruit he was splitting into sections with a cleaver. As she watched him, she noticed a small tattoo on his forearm. She swore it was a hedgehog.

"Just some rich people's show. Always same," he snorted.

Seeing this line of conversation had hit an impasse, she changed tack. "What is that fruit you're preparing? It looks divine!"

He scooped up a few pieces, plopped them into a bowl. He

slid it to Fina across the bar. Then he presented a fork to her as if it were a royal sceptre. "You will love it. Red papaya."

Fina chuckled at herself as the juice dribbled down her chin. "Mmm. You're right!" She saw Lev crack a hint of a smile. She was determined to make friends with him before they arrived in Port of Spain.

"How many times have you been on this voyage, Lev? Were you born in the Bahamas?" she enquired, though she knew he must be from elsewhere.

He answered without looking up from grating lemons. "Oh, more times than I remember. I came to the Bahamas many years ago, from Ukraine."

Ukraine. Fina's auditory nerves suddenly became more acute.

"I see. The Bahamas must be an unusual destination for Ukrainians," she stated, hoping it would prompt an answer.

Silence. He moved on to slicing limes.

Despite the frostiness emanating from her now-taciturn conversation partner, Fina wiped her brow and began to fan herself with the passenger manifest. This action seemed to attract Balraj, and he strode over to Fina like a moth to a flame. While she was relieved to not have to continue the awkward silence, Balraj's sudden attention was equally disconcerting.

Ice clinked in Balraj's glass as he set it on the bar. He turned his full attention to Fina. Lev scowled as if Balraj had left dirty dishes on his personal dining table. Balraj, however, seemed wholly unaware of his surroundings as he came up very close to Fina.

"You must be the famous Miss Dove," he said. His breath tickled her cheek. She stepped back. Fina knew she had an exaggerated need for her own personal space. She flinched as she remembered how the police constables had breathed on her as they interrogated her about her father's death.

Lost in her memories, Fina stepped back too far and hit her shoulder against the railing. Returning to reality, her words began to tumble out. "You must be Mr Chadha. I'm Fina, Fina Aubrey-Havelock. You can just call me Fina. I'm afraid Miss Dove – Ruby, that is – isn't feeling well. She's in her cabin, resting," she said, slowly regaining her composure.

"Pity. I had heard so much about her from my good friend, Gustave. And Dolores told me she was interested in Miss Dove's designs. Please do give her my regards when you see her," he said, now staring at the sea.

"I'm Ruby's assistant, though I am acting as governess on this voyage to little Victor," said Fina.

Suddenly, his head snapped back to Fina with renewed interest.

"Really?" he said, now with even more interest. "Well, I could tell you a few things about your employer, Miss Aubrey-Havelock. Yes, I could indeed." He rubbed his hands together as if he were a small child ready to open birthday gifts. "May I call you Fina? You may certainly call me Balraj."

"Yes, please do call me Fina, ah, Balraj. I must say that you were quite good in *Sapphire Moon*."

"Thank you, dear lady. Though I fear that film was rather, well, shall we say, unsatisfying?"

"Oh, I enjoyed it thoroughly."

"But surely you must have noticed my role was a hopeless caricature."

There it was again, thought Fina. Blast it. Those stinging, warm pinpricks, climbing and lacing their way up her neck. Nothing she could do to stop it. Especially because she felt ashamed.

"Oh, you're right, of course. I didn't even think of it, but you're right. It was quite awful. I suppose I'm so used to those bit parts in films that I just ignore them – but I shouldn't, of course."

Balraj bestowed a broad smile on Fina. "My dear Fina, what a refreshing attitude. Mostly I tell white Britishers that just to make them uncomfortable," he said pausing to take a sip of his drink. "Most of the time they respond with extreme denial and defensiveness. But you were honest."

Fina felt the heat even more intensely in her face now. She took in a big gulp of the salty warm air. "Ah, well, I..." she mumbled.

"I'm actually on a campaign to make the British film industry improve their portrayals of my people. That's why I've been out of work for a while," he said, running his fingers through his long hair.

"Is this an enforced holiday of sorts for you then?" asked Fina.

His relaxed posture vanished, along with his easy charm.

"I suppose you could say that."

The gliding approach of a dapper gentleman saved her from responding to Balraj. The man's carriage was so straight that Fina wondered if he had been in the military. The blue stripes of a sailor's shirt peeked out from underneath the cool white of his suit.

"Let me introduce myself," he said with a little bow to Fina and Balraj. "My name is Maxwell Mills. I am your captain on this voyage. I make a point of personally inviting all of our guests to dinner on the first night aboard. Please follow me to the dining room."

9

"How are you feeling?" Fina queried, lowering herself gently on the bed next to Ruby's huddled figure.

"Mmph. Awful," she whispered in reply.

"So sorry," said Fina, patting her arm under the covers. "Do you want to listen to my report or shall I save it for tomorrow?"

Ruby groaned, but nodded what seemed to be her head in assent. It was difficult to tell since she lay in a foetal position beneath heaps of blankets.

Fina shared her encounters, with special attention to the Sadie-Balraj drama. As she talked, she scribbled notes in her tiny green notebook. Ruby had given it to her as a special gift after the close of their "case" at Pauncefort Hall.

Tap, tap.

"Must be our dinner," said Fina. "I asked for it to be brought down, since I didn't want to desert you for the dining room. Frankly, I'm glad I did. The atmosphere at drinks was rather uncomfortable – positively strained."

Fina opened the door to a petite, spritely woman. Her hair was tied back into a serviceable bun and, like Sadie, she had a number of bangles on her wrist. An onyx apron that had seen better days dampened the warmth of her orange shirt-dress.

She held a tray piled with mounds of food. The sea air fused with the heady smells of celery, onions, tomatoes and rice, automatically bringing a smile to Fina's face. And her stomach grumbled appreciatively as if in answer to this food offering.

"I'm Sarah, Miss Sarah Breeze," said the woman as she handed the tray over to Fina. "I'm the cook on this ship. I heard Miss Dove had a turn, so I made some special food for her. I made sure not to bring any food that has a strong smell. Like fish."

"Most kind of you, Miss Breeze. I'm sure you must be quite busy with the dinner service."

"Wasn't nothing at all," she said with a friendly voice, though she did not smile. She nearly pushed pass Fina to go over to the huddled figure on the bed. She sat down next to Ruby and, reaching into her apron pocket, pulled out a small green bottle and a spoon. She craned her neck around to look at Fina.

"Give her three spoons of this every two hours until she feels better," she said, plopping down the bottle on the nightstand with such force that the orders were clear.

Moans of protestation, incomprehensible, came from the figure on the bed.

"Now don't be fussy, Miss Dove. I know all about seasickness. And that's what you have," she said, chiding Ruby, while eyeing Fina expectantly.

Fina nodded at Sarah as she gently began to remove items from the tray. She moved slowly, afraid that the mounds of food might topple over onto the floor.

Though Sarah's sentences were direct and short, Fina had the sense that she wanted to talk. Well, she could certainly indulge her. After all, she was a consummate listener herself.

"I met Agnes Gidge earlier," said Fina, taking a quick bite of a soft round disc on one of the plates. Mmm. Heaven, she thought.

Sarah rolled her eyes and slid her bracelets up and down her arm. "Ah yes, Agnes. She's a good maid, and she can draw a picture like no one I've ever seen, but what a tongue. Talks all day and night. I'd never be able to cook anything if I didn't tell her to be quiet."

"She did seem rather loquacious," said Fina with a smile. "This is so delicious, Miss Breeze. What is it?" she said, holding up one of the discs with a fork.

"That's just plantain. You Brits love your plantains."

In between enthusiastic bites, Fina asked, "Miss Gidge told me you're quite the poet. Do you write for yourself or ever share it?"

Even though her hands were covered by her apron, Fina could see them tighten into little balls. "That Agnes. The girl's mouth is the size of the whole blue sea."

"Oh, I'm sorry, Miss Breeze, I didn't mean anything by it. I'm always interested in what people do – besides their jobs," said Fina, softly.

The little fists relaxed, but Sarah stood up to go. "Please do remember to give Miss Dove the tonic I left you on the nightstand. And you can leave the tray outside your door. Someone will come by to pick it up."

And with that, she slipped out of the room.

Ruby turned over to gaze at Fina with eyelids at half-mast. With great effort, she said, "Feens, I need you to do something for me."

Ruby reached out to the nightstand and grasped at a piece of folded paper. "Can you slip this under Ian's door?" she said, panting from the effort of lifting her arm. "There must be envelopes in the writing desk."

Doing as she was bidden, Fina fetched an envelope, slipped the piece of paper inside and sealed it. "There," she said with finality. "I need to look in on Victor and Sadie to see if I should read him a bedtime story. The night air will be refreshing."

She fought her fierce curiosity to ask about the note. When it came to Ian, Ruby was as defensive as a cat backed into a corner.

Ruby's only reply was to give her a half-hearted "thank-you" smile. Then she rolled over. Little soft snoring sounds soon came from the pile of blankets. Fina grinned to herself.

She slid the envelope into her favourite clutch. On her way out of the cabin, she snatched one more of those delicious plantains.

She tapped lightly on the door of Sadie and Victor's cabin, not wanting to disturb them in case he was asleep. Licking her sticky fingers, she paused to take in twilight at sea. Weak moonlight filtered through the clouds. A persistent cool breeze ruffled her hair.

If she listened carefully, she could hear the sounds of chairs scraping, laughing and general chatter from above. They must be finishing dinner, she thought. She must hurry in case Ian decided to return to his cabin.

A perfect silence came from Sadie's cabin after her knock, so Fina half walked, half scampered down the deck toward Ian's cabin, number 5.

Suddenly, just as she was about to enter the lounge, a high-pitched screech came from the cabin on her left. It was a scream of shock and fear.

"Ouch!" yelped Fina as she twisted her ankle in surprise.

She limped over to the cabin door and began to knock. Before she had even rapped twice, the door opened abruptly and she almost fell head over heels into the cabin.

Another screech issued from the open mouth of Emeline,

who had flung open the door. Pushing past Fina, she sprinted out of the room, running down the deck.

Fina poked her head around the door.

Then she saw it.

10

"*Mon Dieu!*" bellowed a voice. It was Gustave, who had crept up right behind Fina. "What was that catastrophic rumpus? Ah – it makes my head ache! It sounded like a shrieking swine!" Fina was rooted to the spot, unable to move away from the doorway.

A small, inky, crab-like creature scuttled across the bedclothes and leapt onto the floor.

That was enough for Fina. She spun round and dashed down the darkened deck toward the lounge, then skidded to a halt as she ran straight into the arms of Ian.

He grabbed her and she responded with a hug. She scanned his face and could see by those furrowed eyebrows that he was concerned about more than her well-being. Was it just her fancy or did she see a look of fear in his eyes?

"Oh, Ian! There's some horrible creature in Emeline and Patricia's room. The scream you heard was from Emeline. She must have seen it come out from one of the beds!"

She turned back toward the cabin, afraid she might see the creature again. Ian held her as she turned. A small crowd had gathered, including a trembling Emeline. She was taking care to stay safely within the pool of light that spilled out from the open doorway. Lev emerged, grimly triumphant, with a jar. Fina was relieved the jar was opaque.

The captain exited the room and removed his cap. "Dear guests. Do not trouble yourselves with worry. A scorpion may sometimes find its way aboard a ship, but we have never found one in a guest cabin. Perhaps it attached itself to Miss Caulk's luggage."

Emeline scowled at Captain Mills. She looked rather dubious, but that was how she always looked, thought Fina.

Ian said in a soft voice, "What colour was it, Fina?"

"Inky black."

"Hmm. Might be *Tityus trinitatis*. They are found mostly in Trinidad. Scorpions do bite, but are usually not lethal. Except for *Tityus trinitatis*. It's blessed luck Miss Caulk discovered it before retiring for bed."

Fina began to shake all over. She often had recurring nightmares where she felt insects crawling on her – so seemingly real that they would awake her in the night.

Ian wrapped her tightly in her shawl. He withdrew a small flask from his pocket and said, "Here, take a sip of this. It will calm your nerves and help you to sleep. I'll need some myself – I am afraid of insects and spiders... and scorpions generally fall into that category."

The sweet liquid fire burned her throat. She coughed and smiled.

"Never had rum, have you?" he said with a laugh.

She laughed along with him. "I have now. It's not bad. I could get used to it."

As they walked down the deck past the huddled crowd, Fina turned to give him the envelope.

"I was supposed to slip this under your door. I don't see a need for secrecy since you'll know it's from Ruby in any case."

"How is she?"

"She insists it is a touch of the flu, but I think it's seasickness. One of the staff gave her a tonic for it."

Suddenly Ian grabbed her arm. A bit too tightly. "Which member of the staff?"

"The cook. Sarah Breeze."

He let go of her arm. "So sorry, I didn't mean to squeeze so hard. I was just – worried, that's all. You know I care about Ruby. Even though she is cross with me."

"Yes, I know that, Ian. But you must see that this whole scenario seems rather, well, dashed odd." Fina decided to take the plunge. She was blunt more often than not on accident – why not do it on purpose for once?

"Why *are* you here, Ian?"

He stared out over the railing, not looking at her. "I'm afraid, Fina. I'm afraid."

And with that, he spun on his heel and melted into the sombre fog that had crept onto the deck.

11

"Pass the marmalade, will you, Feens?" asked Ruby.

Mumbling a garbled "yes" in between forkfuls of eggs, Fina slid the clear jar across to Ruby. The orange gelatinous substance quivered from the motion of the sea.

As if answering an unasked question, Ruby said, "I think I can just manage some toast and perhaps a coffee. With loads of cream, of course."

Fina grinned at Ruby, whose face had almost recovered its normal colour, in contrast to the shades of grey it had assumed last night. The tonic had worked wonders. Ruby's dark blue silk dressing-gown-combination-frock seemed to fit her mellow, reflective mood.

Fina's introspective side had gone into overdrive as well. Though she had already felt what one might term "an atmosphere" yesterday, the terrifying scorpion incident only confirmed it. What did it all mean? Could the scorpion be connected to their mission? Surely *that* couldn't be the hint or clue sent to them. And, as usual, she turned back to her food to soothe her nerves.

"Could you pass me a plantain? Or maybe two? I think I'll eat myself silly on this trip."

"Don't worry – you'll soon be sick of plantains by the time we return to Oxford! Though they are lovely and I have missed them."

With few occupants, the dining room was quiet and peaceful, striped by bars of sunlight slipping through the slatted wooden blinds. Nevertheless, a crunching sound interrupted their desultory exchange. Emeline Caulk shook the newspaper she held in front of her face as if it would shield her from their conversation. It was an effective device. She had uttered no more than two words to them since she had marched into breakfast. Fina tried to be compassionate – must be the poor woman's nerves. Who wouldn't be taciturn after finding a scorpion in their cabin?

She shivered again, brushing her neck to make sure insects hadn't somehow crept up her shoulder.

As she hadn't had a chance to read that same newspaper when she'd picked it up in the lounge, Fina let her eyes roam over the headlines held up across from her. "Loch Ness Monster Hoax". "Hollywood Scandal". "London Banking Embezzlement Scheme – Thousands of Pounds Missing – Police Seek Top Bank Worker". Good Lord. No wonder it felt good to ignore the news.

Fina sensed a consummate consumer of gossip sat behind that newspaper. She decided to save her more secretive questions for Ruby until later.

"Are you going to work with Gustave today?"

"Yes. Dolores wants to look at some sketches, so I'll need to see what I can pull together in a few hours' time. I think I'm feeling up to it now."

The scraping of chair legs next to her indicated a new visitor had arrived at their rather pathetic party.

"Good morning, Miss Aubrey-Havelock. And good morning

to you – you must be Miss Dove. I've heard so much about you," intoned Balraj. Though he retained his charming manner and handsome dishevelled look, Fina noticed that his jaw made little rhythmic popping motions, in and out. Without taking his eyes off Ruby, he helped himself to a piece of toast.

"How alarming!" Ruby said with a deprecating giggle. "It is indeed a pleasure to meet you, Mr Chadha. I am a consummate fan of your work. And I admire you greatly for your stand against the film industry."

He positively glowed with pleasure. "You know all about that, do you? Well, we will have to talk soon – in more depth, I hope."

Selkies and kelpies, thought Fina. He's laying it on rather thick. Balraj leaned across the table and stared intently at Ruby's face.

As if he could sense any advance on Ruby, Ian materialised out of nowhere, casual as ever in a light blue linen suit.

"I hope I'm not interrupting," he said, clearly meaning exactly the opposite. He moved closer to Ruby.

Ruby let out an audible sigh. She glanced at Fina with an exasperated look.

She was saved from taking any action by the entrance of a small boy.

"Fina!" Victor yelped as he rushed to Fina's side. "Come quickly!"

She hurriedly pushed back her chair from the table and joined Victor on deck. Great spurts of water emanated from the calm sea like confetti into the morning air. "There's another one!" shouted Victor, jumping up and down. "Golly! And another!" Fina was concerned he might wet himself from the excitement.

Though his initial cries of alarm to her made her heart nearly leap out of her chest, she could not be cross with him.

The whales were rather marvellous, she thought. They slowly loped along next to the boat at an unhurried clip.

"Look! A baby!" he cried. Fina had to restrain him, otherwise she was sure he would have jumped overboard to join the whales on their morning jaunt. Naturally, Gilbert had heard his squeals and raced over instantly to join in the cheering squad. Lev and Neville were now by the children's side, handing them small field glasses to examine their friends more closely.

A small crowd materialised around the children. They were all a delighted, joyful family for a few brief moments on the ship. Fina knew the squabbles, jealousies and insecurities would rise up in a few moments again – just as sure as the whales would continue their rhythmic spouts.

As expected, as soon as the whales had decided they had better plans than to perform for the ship, Fina heard a "tsk, tsk" sound from behind her. She craned her neck around, reluctantly, to see who could disapprove of such a joyful moment.

It was Patricia, tall and austere, dressed in a delightful white suit with a matching hat. Her lapel held a beautiful cameo brooch. She wore matching dangling cameo earrings. Fina wondered if these cameos were Patricia's lucky charms, given her interest in spiritualism. Beneath her hat, her perfect hair was twisted and curved like ocean waves in a Japanese woodcut panel.

She moved closer to Fina, propelled as if by an unseen force. Fina backed up against the railing. It was impossible to relax with this woman looming over her.

"Have you seen the whales, Mrs Burbage? They could be humpbacks, perhaps... do you suppose?"

With a sniff, Patricia dismissed the whales. "Miss Aubrey-Havelock. I had hoped to find you with your friend, Miss Dove. There's something I wish to speak to you both about. It's a matter of some urgency." She glanced around conspiratorially, earrings swinging. "A *confidential* matter."

"I see," said Fina, as her fingers and arms began to tingle with anticipation. Perhaps this would be related to the charged exchange of glances she had seen pass between Patricia and Sadie the previous evening. Out of the corner of her eye, she saw Ruby's graceful form approaching from the dining room. "Here she comes now. Shall we take a turn about the deck?"

Patricia looked around once more. The whale-watchers had dispersed, and the faint clatter of cutlery suggested that most of the other passengers were safely occupied at breakfast.

"By all means," she said curtly, turning toward Ruby. "If you're agreeable, Miss Dove?"

"Delighted," said Ruby, clearly not sure what she was agreeing to. She raised an inquisitive eyebrow at Fina. Fina waggled her head and winked in a way that tried to convey that she should play along. Ruby seemed to get the message.

As they started off, Patricia took a deep, trembling breath. Her self-assurance, so valiantly maintained in front of the other passengers, was showing some cracks now that she was out of the public eye. She was clearly desperate to open up to someone, thought Fina. And yet no words were forthcoming.

"Er, is there something we can help you with, perhaps, Mrs Burbage?" Fina asked at last.

Patricia gripped the brass rail that enclosed the deck. "It's true that I do have a predicament. But it's very hard to put into words." She paused to adjust her hat, which had been nudged askew by the warm breeze. "Tell me, have either of you by any chance noticed any sort of – well, what you might call an *atmosphere* on board this ship?"

Beside her, Fina felt Ruby prick up her ears. Patricia was oblivious.

"It's interesting you should say that," replied Ruby. "Now that you mention it, there has been some tension among the passengers. My friend and I have some experience in investigation, so —" she gave Fina a sidelong glance "—we're very sensitive to such things."

"So you are investigators! I thought as much," said Patricia. Even in the midst of her anxiety, she still managed to sound smug, thought Fina. "I can always tell," she went on. "You see, I've had occasion to hire investigators several times in the past. My husband's oil business was a very lucrative one. And great wealth always tends to attract scoundrels. It brings out the worst in people. Of course, that's something you'll know all about, given your sleuthing experience." Her mouth twisted into a thin smile. It seemed that her wide experience of investigators had not supplied a high opinion of the profession.

"Quite," said Ruby in an equally chilly tone. Her footsteps quickened, tapping impatiently on the planks. "Please note that we are not professionals, by any means. My time is mostly taken up with my chemistry studies at Oxford, and Fina is in the same college, reading history. But let's get back to the voyage, shall we, Mrs Burbage? What exactly is worrying you about this trip?"

The thin smile vanished and Patricia took another shuddering breath. She turned to Fina. "You were there last night – you saw what happened."

"The scorpion, yes." Fina shivered in sympathy. "I can't help but feel you and your sister were lucky. That could have been a nasty accident."

"Accident?" Patricia gave another of her dismissive sniffs. "That was no accident. That scorpion was planted in my bed on purpose!"

Ruby and Fina exchanged glances. "But why would someone do such a thing?" asked Fina.

Lowering her voice, Patricia leaned in closer. She removed her sunglasses and pointed the tip of one of the arms at Ruby.

"Because someone is trying to kill me – and that someone is on board this ship at this very moment. I'm certain of it."

They had reached the bow, and all three paused to watch the prow of the ship cut cleanly through the cerulean water. Behind Patricia's back, Ruby tilted her head sideways as if to communicate to Fina that clearly, the woman was suffering from heatstroke. "I'm sorry, Mrs Burbage. Do you have any evidence for this belief?"

"Tsk tsk," clicked Patricia. "I don't need fingerprints or cigarash to tell me when I'm being persecuted. My late husband was a very shrewd man, and back in Canada, he made a great many enemies in the course of his career – ignorant people who don't understand the way the oil business works. It's not like running a nursery school, for goodness' sake," she said with another sniff. "Naturally, some of those people have carried a grudge ever since. There have been other attempts on my life: last year, my chauffeur found the brake cables on my car had been cut – *cut!* – and I've had several attacks of food poisoning that my doctor considered to be extremely suspect. But there has been none so audacious as this one."

She paused for breath and seemed to regain a measure of confidence.

"Now that you're aware of the facts," she went on, "you'll be able to protect me and identify the perpetrator. I trust that won't take you long?"

That's torn it, thought Fina. Ruby whirled around, nearly knocking over Patricia as she did so, as if to emphasise the point that she was standing too close to them.

"Mrs Burbage. As I've said, we are not investigators. We are here on holiday – holiday mixed with other work. We are not at your disposal. Let me be clear. Just because you believe you are being targeted does not mean I, or rather we, share your opinion. Now, if you have specific information you'd like us to pass along to Captain Mills, we would be happy to do so, though I cannot imagine why you wouldn't talk to him in the first place."

Patricia recoiled, drawing her chin back with a haughty glare.

"If I had wanted to approach the captain, you may be sure I would have done so already," she retorted. "Miss Dove, I will leave the matter in your hands. But I can assure you it would be in your best interest to reconsider." Adjusting her hat once more, she stalked off down the opposite side of the ship.

"Phew!" Ruby shuddered. "If anyone deserves a beast in their bed, it's her. I am so glad I missed that episode. I don't like anything that crawls or scuttles."

"It was ghastly. And why would anyone use a scorpion as a murder weapon? Do you think it could have wandered onto the ship and into her room by mistake? All the doors were unlocked when we came on board."

"Could it have attached itself to someone's luggage? I don't know anything about scorpions, but it does strike me as a dubious explanation."

"Possibly, but I wouldn't like to have to suggest it to her myself."

Ruby shook her head ruefully. "Much as I've love to interrogate all our fellow passengers and crew on their feelings about Patricia Burbage, I'm afraid I've got to get back to those designs for Dolores. She asked me to let her have something by lunchtime." Ruby's expression turned introspective, a sure sign that the creative fires were burning. "Feens, do you think she'd look good in yellow? A dark gold type of shade?"

"I don't see why not. That blue she had on yesterday was rather subdued; she could easily handle something more vivid."

"Thanks, dearest. Come and give me your thoughts on the drawings in a little while?"

"I'd love to." But what to do in the meantime? She had fifteen minutes until she was due to pick up Victor. Fina decided to see if anyone was on the quoits deck. Perhaps Ian would give her a quick game.

But just as she reached the stairs to the top deck, a hand tapped her on the shoulder. Not again, she thought. This time it was Emeline. She was dressed, no, encased – again – in a brown material that tried to mimic linen, but failed miserably. Was it burlap? Surely not. But it did look like a cross between tweed and linen.

The hairs on Fina's arm prickled. Just looking at that material made her itch.

"Oh, good morning, Miss Caulk. I don't suppose you fancy a game of quoits?"

"It seems a trivial recreation," huffed Emeline.

"But it is rather an enjoyable way to pass the time on board ship, Miss Caulk. You must admit."

"I will admit no such thing, Miss Aubrey-Havelock,' she said, nose held high.

As if realising she had gone too far, she bent her considerable frame toward Fina in a conspiratorial voice. "I must speak to you urgently, Miss Aubrey-Havelock."

Fina's stomach tensed. She could feel her eyes growing wider. Did Emeline have inside information about the strange atmosphere on the voyage – or the alleged attempt on her sister's life? She wished Ruby hadn't retreated to their cabin. Drat. Well, she could handle this on her own.

Smiling at Emeline – though not for the reason Emeline might have supposed – Fina nodded. "But I am due to have lessons with Victor. May he accompany us? I can ask him to read quietly if we go to the reading room."

Emeline gave her approval with a grimace and a nod. She stormed toward the reading room.

12

A pleasing jumble of books lined the walls of the reading room. They formed a sort of cocoon which eased Fina's nervousness. Nervousness borne of anticipation? Perhaps, but if she were honest with herself, it was also disgust at the woman sitting across from her in the high wingback chair. Victor hummed softly in the corner, alternately reading and playing with his giraffe.

Emeline's face, in contrast to her rigid frame, was quite round – an effect heightened by tightly pulled back hair. Her head appeared completely disembodied, as if it had been borrowed from someone else. The only contribution to fashion was a long string of pearls, falling down her chest as if they were trying to escape to the floor.

Fina broke into a sweat as she studied Emeline's usual high-necked dress. When Emeline bent to the side to pick up her pince-nez that had fallen to the floor, Fina saw an angry-looking scar – a long, pinkish slash across her neck. Well, at least one mystery was solved, thought Fina. She was surprised that Emeline was self-conscious about this scar. She had admired a woman who could so completely not care what other people thought of her.

Placing her pince-nez firmly back on her nose, Emeline clasped her hands in her lap and began to bark out phrases, like a small, rather excited dog.

"Miss Aubrey-Havelock. I need to speak to you. About the boy. About you."

Emeline's hands quivered in her lap. Her arms pressed her hands down deeper into her lap, as if in an epic struggle of will with her hands.

"Yes, Miss Caulk. Do go on. And please call me Fina."

Ignoring her completely, Emeline said, "Miss Aubrey-Have-lock. That boy should not be exposed. Exposed to..." She began to sputter. Little flecks of spit appeared from her lips and quickly dissipated into the ether.

"Yes, Miss Caulk?"

As if giving in to the urge of an addict, Emeline's whole body relaxed as she withdrew a pamphlet from her carpet bag.

Fina's stomach began to flip gently, like an omelette being turned in a pan. This must be it!

She scrutinised the gift from Emeline. The title read *Race Mixing and the Dangers to White Womanhood*. It featured pictures of happy white children on the front cover.

Fina's heart sank. Not only was Emeline clearly not their contact, but she was just as disturbed on the inside as she appeared to be on the outside.

"I saw you talking to the steward. Neville. And. well. You travel with Miss Dove. You know we British women – or I should say we British women of the Empire – have a moral duty to preserve and uphold the race."

Before Fina could respond – which she couldn't because she was frozen in place – Emeline pulled out another pamphlet from her veritable library posing as a carpet bag. She nearly flung it into Fina's lap.

Still dumbfounded, Fina looked down at the second pamphlet. She recognised the title. She had heard about it from friends – it was so controversial that she hadn't seen a copy of it. The title was *Married Love* by Marie Stopes. One of these friends had told her that Stopes advocated compulsory sterilisation. Just the thought of it made her shudder.

Clearly taking advantage of Fina's inanimate state, Emeline leaned over and whispered, "I have some paraphernalia, you know, in my cabin. You should give it most especially to Miss Dove. And for yourself, though I clearly advise you against taking up with that Neville character."

Fina's muscles began to move again. She unclenched her fist and stretched the joints of her fingers. Then, looking down at her now flat, but shaking hand she sprang out of her chair. The offending pamphlets spilled onto the floor.

Without any conscious thought, Fina heard a "thwack" and looked down at the reddening left cheek of Emeline's now bunched up, round face.

Fina glanced briefly at her own red hand, as if in disbelief. She heard her own voice say calmly as she mechanically scooped up her clutch from the chair, "Come, Victor. Perhaps we can see if Gilbert wants to play. It has certainly become much too stuffy in this room. I can hardly breathe. There seems to be a distinct odour which I cannot abide."

Out on deck, Fina sucked in great gulps of tangy air. The gentle lapping of the waves was a welcome relief. She could almost convince herself that Emeline did not exist. Not wanting to tempt fate by allowing her time to follow out of the reading room, she grabbed Victor's hand and led him down the deck toward the Gibbses' cabin. The idea of being wholly immersed in the worries of children rather than adults was most appealing.

"What does it mean to 'uphold the race', Fina?"

Good Lord. The child *had* been listening.

Playing for time, she said, "You know, I definitely want to talk to you about this – but it will take some time. Let's save it for later and see if Gilbert wants to play now."

Victor indicated his agreement by banging on the Gibbses' door.

She heard a scraping sound, followed by the rhythm of little feet sprinting toward the door.

Gilbert flung open the door and gave them a wide grin, revealing a missing front tooth.

"Look! I just lost my tooth. Now I can whistle!" He began to huff and puff, producing a raspy wheeze. Fina was concerned that he might hyperventilate.

"That's lovely, Gilbert. Can you play with Victor?"

"Yes! Mummy and Daddy went upstairs to lay in the sun. I was bored so they let me play in here. Come see my train set, Victor!"

The magic words had been spoken and soon the two boys were engrossed in their train play.

Fina wiped her hand across her forehead. Had she really just slapped Emeline? The good girl voice inside of her immediately arose and asked her why on earth she had resorted to physical violence. Fortunately, Fina recognised this judgment for what it was. She could think about it later. There was work to be done!

It wouldn't hurt to have a peek around the Gibbses' cabin, would it? She convinced herself that Ruby would most certainly approve. Fina began to systematically scan the room, starting by the bedside and moving in a clockwise direction.

The bedside table held glasses of water, a tube of lipstick, a book she didn't recognise and a tin of mints. More of Violet's worn and faded dresses were draped on the bed. Moving methodically into the bathroom, she saw three toothbrushes, night cream, toothpaste, a hairbrush and some sort of hair tonic and gel. Everything was quite orderly here.

Fina felt a magnetic pull toward the writing desk. Perhaps... should she? Of course. Everyone had one of these desks, so it wasn't like prying into their luggage. Under the accusing eye of yet another sandstone parrot sculpture, she slid open the left-hand drawer of the mahogany desk.

"Are you looking for this?"

"Oh, Victor. You nearly made my heart stop!" Fina said in reply to his offer of a small wooden train. She took it, ran it across the desk, making "choo-choo" noises, and then returned it to Victor. Satisfied, he went back to his train engineer duties on the floor.

She told herself that she was just searching for pen and paper. Nothing else. Sliding open the middle drawer, she came across a velvet-covered octagonal box. You really shouldn't, she thought. But perhaps there will be a pen inside?

The box was one of those ones that snap into place like a crocodile's jaw. She prised it open, while still leaving it in the drawer. Her fingers tingled. The box revealed a veritable treasure trove of jewellery. Silver chains snaked through gold rings. None of the gems were particularly large, but the collection was worth a small fortune. More like a large fortune, particularly given what seemed to be the rather genteel poverty of the Gibbses.

Snap. The box shut, almost of its own accord. The sound brought her back to reality. She slammed the drawer, just as she heard voices floating down the deck.

13

"There you are!"

Phillip Gibbs trotted into the room, looking tanned in his one-piece swimming costume. Perhaps it was the lighting. An insouciant towel was draped over one half-naked shoulder. It somehow complemented the pipe he clutched in his mouth.

"Glad to see the two young chaps are getting on," he said, grinning at Fina. Fina was nearly sitting on the desk – as if she could cover her discovery. "We've had a marvellous sunbathing session, haven't we, Vi?" Fina thought the statement was too broad. "I" instead of "we" would have been more appropriate. Violet, who had plod in behind her husband, must have had on a bathing costume. If so, however, it was difficult to see it beneath the layers – or large strips – of cotton. Her pastiness was even more pronounced than it had been yesterday.

"Mmm. Yes, dear," she said absently, flopping down in the chair nearest to Fina. "Gilbert? Have you been behaving yourself for Miss Aubrey-Havelock?"

Fina rescued Gilbert from having to answer. "He's been delightful. They've been completely engrossed in their trains." She paused. She could feel the heaviness in the room. And it wasn't simply due to her own discovery in the desk. "Would you mind awfully if I left the boys to play? I promised Ruby I would find her soon."

"Certainly, Miss Aubrey-Havelock. We'll look after him. We've already chatted with Lady Winchcombe-Twisleton about Victor."

And with that, Fina left the oppressive tension of the Gibbses' abode. She strolled around the deck toward the bow, stopping to admire the blue of the sea. The blue was so brilliant it looked artificial. A late lunch buffet had been set up under an awning, and she tucked into a plate of food with relish.

As she put down her fork, she turned and saw an easy, lanky figure walking toward her in a striped shirt. A cigarette hung out of his mouth – looking like it was trying to escape, unsuccessfully.

Neville.

She felt heat creeping up her neck – and it was not just due to the afternoon sunshine. Emeline's earlier comments about Neville made her feel decidedly self-conscious.

Roughly paralleling Neville on the other side of the deck, she saw Ruby and Dolores approaching her. Fina relaxed. She wasn't afraid of being alone with Neville – quite the contrary – but she somehow felt relieved by their appearance.

The two women nattered away, pointing from time to time at what Fina presumed to be sketches in Ruby's book. Dolores was also smoking, though this time through a jade green holder which she held languidly by her side. When she used her hands to make a point to Ruby, the cigarette let off little circles of smoke around her head.

Neville reached her first. He looked down at Fina, gravely, as if she was about to be scolded. Perhaps it was just because of the angle of the sun? "Hello, Miss Aubrey-Havelock. How are you enjoying the books I recommended yesterday?"

"I, I haven't had the chance to begin them yet."

"Begin what?" Dolores queried, delicately tapping her cigarette holder on the rail to release the ash into the sea. Instead of navy, she had lightened up a bit with a grey, form-fitting shift. Her sandals were her nod to the humidity. She was wearing round, almost completely opaque sunglasses. Fina wasn't accustomed to talking to people wearing sunglasses – especially given the ever-so-sunny British weather. She found it disconcerting not to be able to look at someone's eyes.

"Ah, we were just discussing Neville's book recommendations."

"My, how intriguing," she said, with a throaty laugh that reminded Fina of those sheets used to make thunder noise in a radio play. She slowly straightened her spine. She already had quite an incredible posture, so this seemed like a special feat. "Your friend, dear Ruby, has been sharing delightful sketches with me. I look forward to having these – what do you call them – *frocks* made when we arrive in Port of Spain. Gustave has recommended someone to me, since I know you and Ruby have other plans when you arrive."

Somehow, out of the ether, Balraj had joined their little party.

"But dear Dolores. You know you should not be seen," he said with a rather mischievous grin.

Though Fina could not see Dolores' eyes behind the sunglasses, the puckering disapproval of her mouth spoke volumes.

Ruby intervened. "Oh, I'm sure we can make an arrangement to sew the garments so you won't need to leave the hotel. I'm quite certain Gustave can assist with that."

Dolores nodded gratefully in her direction. She sat down on a nearby wicker chair and looked out to sea.

There was a tranquil pause, broken only by the arrival of the

Gibbses. Phillip had changed into a seemlier white shirt and trousers, while Violet had draped herself in yet more layers of cotton.

"Mummy, Mummy!" came Gilbert's piping voice. "May I have an ice? You said I could if it was a hot day!"

Violet's answering look at her son was half affection, half exasperation. "All right, darling. Ask the man over there."

Yipping with delight, Gilbert bounded over to Neville. "Please, sir," he said. "Could I have a bowl with all your ices? All kinds? With sprinkles? And marshmallows?"

His parents exchanged appalled glances. Violet, it seemed, could hardly stop herself from shouting. "Er, no, darling," she finally said, managing to keep her voice level. "That's rather more than we can manage on this trip. Perhaps you could have something a little simpler. A strawberry ice, for instance?" Without waiting for Gilbert's response, she turned to Neville. "Could he have one strawberry ice, please, and no toppings."

"Right away, ma'am," said Neville, with a sympathetic grin at Gilbert.

Gilbert, torn between disappointment and relief that he was getting anything at all, grinned back. Phillip's expression, though, was riven with anxiety as he glanced around the assembled company.

It was odd, Fina reflected, that a family who could afford to splash out so lavishly on jewellery would be penny-pinching over small matters. The cost of their ticket from England to Port of Spain must not have been cheap, either. If they could afford to come out here, just for a holiday, presumably they could afford the occasional sugary treat for their son.

Soon, to Gilbert's joy, the ice lolly arrived. He tucked in without any self-consciousness, but his parents, aware that his little drama had been overheard by everyone, guided him to the upper deck in retreat.

Balraj shifted on his feet and took a great gulp of his cocktail. "Do you all find that couple odd – what is their name?" he asked, speaking to no one in particular.

"Gibbs, sir," said Neville.

"Ah yes. Gibbs," replied Balraj. He scratched his jaw in a gesture of puzzlement. "As I said, something dashed odd about them."

Silence. Everyone must be waiting for him to elaborate or didn't want to engage in the conversation, thought Fina.

Ruby snapped her notebook shut.

A sudden great breeze ruffled her dress and nearly toppled Ruby's large sun hat.

Neville cleared his throat. "I came to tell Miss Aubrey-Havelock the news, but as you're all here, I can report it to you." He pointed over the railing to a great raft of Devonshire cream clouds, puffing out and up into tall, furry-looking pillars.

"A storm is brewing. The captain will do his best to avoid it, but it will put us a bit behind schedule. It also means that we have decided to cancel drinks at the bar and have an early dinner instead."

They all stared at the clouds that seemed so out of place with the general blue, cloudless calm all around them.

"That must mean it's time for another drink!" proclaimed Balraj, nearly sliding away down the deck toward the stairs.

Dolores stood up, removed her cigarette stub from the holder and flung it into the sea. "Thank you for a delightful afternoon, and your delightful sketches, dear Ruby. You are a treasure." She touched her head with a rather theatrical gesture. Well, she was an actress, after all, thought Fina. "I have a headache, so I don't know if I'll join you all for dinner. Please forgive me."

As she made her exit, Fina saw Emeline and Patricia whispering in two of the lounge chairs. By the looks they gave to

Dolores, she thought they must be gossiping about her. Patricia sucked on the straw in her pink cocktail, nearly draining the glass. Emeline sipped from a teacup. Feeling protective of Neville, she decided she'd better be the one to tell the two women about the impending storm.

Ruby was now engaged in conversation with Neville, so she tapped her on the shoulder. "I need to talk to Emeline and Patricia. How about we meet in the green room in a few minutes?"

"Good idea. Our cabin is stifling. I'll be there soon."

Fina turned toward Emeline and Patricia, when waves of the cocktail jolted out of Patricia's glass, splattering her beautiful white summer dress.

"You fool!" she yelled at Emeline, in a voice considerably louder than Fina had heard from her so far.

"So sorry, Patty," said Emeline. But she did not get up from her chair to help mend the damage. She was frozen in place.

Neville was by their side in a flash. "Here, let me help you, Mrs Burbage," he said, offering her a large handkerchief.

She waved her hand away at him, as if he were a mosquito. One that was flying perilously close to the juiciest part of her arm. "No, please. I'll take care of it," she said, rising and nearly running off in the direction of her cabin.

Emeline had thawed from her frozen state, but did not look inclined to go after her sister.

Fina broke the silence. "Miss Caulk, the captain has informed us that there will be a storm falling shortly. He has advised us that we should have an early dinner and dispose of the usual cocktail hour."

Without looking up from her teacup, she responded, "Drink is the devil's playground, Miss Aubrey-Havelock. I'm glad to hear the captain has made a sound choice."

As if in response, the ship's foghorn sounded.

14

The green room was blessedly empty, except for Gustave and Sadie huddled in chairs near the bar. Fina admired Sadie's double-breasted yellow and orange beach dress. She and Gustave spoke in a relaxed, amiable way – the way one does when one doesn't really know someone yet, but wants to be polite.

A long, shining bar stood at one end of the room and windows at the other. The light from the windows – as much as it was waning given the oncoming storm – brought a welcome airiness to the heavy Edwardian furniture. Blues and pink hues emanated from thickly painted, framed canvases scattered about the room.

"Gin and tonic, please," said Fina to Lev. Lev appeared completely relaxed in his striped sailor's shirt.

"And a pink gin for me, please," said Ruby. Though Ruby had fully recovered from her *mal de mer*, she looked a little, what was it? Haunted? Perhaps it was just the circles under her eyes.

Fina shivered with pleasure at the cool tartness of the gin mixed with the sweet bubbles of the tonic.

"I feel much better now."

"Let's sit by the windows," said Ruby, with a nod of thanks to Lev for her drink.

Ruby pushed together two chairs so their arms touched. They faced the rest of the bar so they could keep an eye on the comings and goings.

Ruby rubbed her arm. "I can tell a storm is coming. I'm getting little shock waves of electricity. Feels like the hair is standing up on my arm."

Fina nodded with sympathy. One of her cousins had this same trait of being extra sensitive to electric storms. Her own body shivered, as if in sympathy. She pulled a shawl from her handbag and wound it around her arms. She could see from the barometer in the corner that the pressure was dropping quickly.

"Let's talk. I'm afraid this storm will provoke another round of seasickness for me! I'll take extra precautions when we dress for dinner – I'll double up – no, I'll triple up – on the tonic dosage. I must thank Sarah for her gift. It truly has been a gift."

"Mmm," said Fina, as an affirmative response through a sip of her drink. She munched on some nuts from a bowl on the table. "I'll tell you about what I've found out so far." She relayed to Ruby everything about Emeline, the Gibbses and Neville.

"My, I am impressed," said Ruby, sitting back in her chair. "I mean, I'm impressed by everything that you've found, but I just cannot believe that you slapped Emeline!"

Ruby began to chuckle. And then the chuckle turned into laughter. Gustave and Sadie looked over at them. Ruby suppressed the noise but still smiled at Fina.

Fina began to giggle. "Yes, well, you know I can be impulsive. But as my grandmother said, where the tongue slips, it speaks the truth."

"Very true! And speaking of truth, I think we can safely dismiss everything Patricia was telling us after breakfast today, don't you?"

"I do. It sounded like a story you'd read in one of those pulp fiction novelettes. After all, a scorpion planted in someone's bed is hardly a reliable murder weapon."

"She clearly believes it all herself, of course," said Ruby thoughtfully. "And it may well be true that there are financers or others who bore a grudge against her husband. But if so, why would they hold on to such a grudge even after his death, and transfer it to his widow? It's not her fault if he made some ruthless decisions."

"Delusions of grandeur," said Fina decisively.

"She certainly does have a high opinion of herself." Ruby shifted in her seat and crossed her legs. "So it seems everyone on board has, well, shall we say, certain proclivities – as a generous interpretation – but none of them seem to fit with the letter we received. Or do they?"

Fina tilted her head back against the chair. She stared at the hairline crack in the ceiling. "Well, the only thing that seems likely is the fact that Neville mentioned his reading recommendations again. That seems significant."

"Go on," said Ruby, sipping her gin. She grimaced slightly, a grimace that turned into a slow smile of satisfaction.

"Well, that's it, really. It just seems important. But I cannot figure out the angle. You took a look at the Makhno book he gave me, didn't you?"

"Yes, I skimmed it. There aren't any significant markings in the book. It cannot be the text itself, could it?"

"Perhaps, but that is rather vague. How did you get on this morning?"

Ruby sighed. "It depends on which area you're talking about. As for design, it was enormously edifying to be recognised as a real designer – for once – by Dolores. We sat in her cabin and chatted and sketched, sketched and chatted. She is rather shy for an actor. But then again, what do I really know about that!"

Ruby stared into her glass. Then she began to tap her teeth.

"I know that look. Did something else happen?"

She bit her lip, as if holding back a secret. Then her teeth released her lip. "I'm not sure, but there was something peculiar. She kept referring to 'we' when describing what she would do on the ship or in Trinidad, but would quickly slip back into 'I' as if she had made an embarrassing mistake."

"Do you think she has a lover? But why would she be embarrassed? She's a liberated Hollywood actress, after all."

"That's what's odd. It's also odd because she didn't seem, well, bashful. She seemed a little afraid."

"Afraid of someone?"

"Could be. But it could also be she was afraid *for* someone. But that was just an impression," Ruby said, relaxing back into the chair.

Fina couldn't help asking, "And the designs?"

Ruby's smile had a touch of professional pride. "Most of them she loved. The evening gowns in particular: she loved the one with the dramatic neckline." Then the smile vanished. "There was one thing, though."

"What?"

"Well, I brought along a few of Gustave's designs as well, since we're meant to be a team. And frankly, they were almost..." She tapped her teeth. "Almost amateurish. He's clearly talented, but on the practical side, he's severely lacking. It's almost as if he's forgotten all his training. Any back-street tailor would know that you'd never get organza to drape in such a way."

"How odd," said Fina. Still, it wouldn't be the first time the Parisian *haute monde* had celebrated a creative talent far in excess of his or her abilities.

"As for our other task, I came across this," Ruby said, opening her clutch to reveal a folded-up newspaper. She handed it over to Fina.

It was *The New York Times*, the same 3rd May issue that Fina had seen Emeline reading.

Fina read aloud: "Actress Blacklisted."

"I dislike that term intensely," said Ruby. "It should be 'whitelisted'."

Fina didn't understand her meaning at first, but the message slowly dawned on her.

"You mean terms like 'black-something' should be avoided or replaced?" She felt enormously naive as soon as she uttered the question.

Ruby looked undisturbed. "Yes. Think about all the negative terms associated with the word 'black', such as 'blackmail' or 'blackballed'." She smiled. "Sorry to be pedantic, Feens."

"No, no, no need to apologise. I hadn't thought of it before." With that she began to read:

Hollywood executives have decried actress Dolores Dominguez's accusations of inappropriate conduct with young extras on film sets. Miss Dominguez, famous for her roles in Blue Hyacinths and Three Teardrops, previously reported to The New York Times that three Hollywood executives regularly took "liberties" with young actresses on the set. When pressed further, she said that some of these women had told her that these men had violated them.

Miss Dominguez has declined to name the specific executives involved. She said she "fears for these women's safety" if she were to name the men involved...

The article continued, but the main point was clear to Fina. She gave a low whistle. "It's certainly salacious, but what does it have to do with us?"

"Though the reason is somewhat foggy, it does offer a possible reason why Dolores is travelling to Trinidad."

Fina blinked.

"I think it makes it unlikely that she is our contact. It seemed odd at first that someone of her stature would be taking this trip with us. Now it provides a possible explanation – that she is hiding or on the run, but not necessarily our contact."

"I see. You're eliminating possible contacts, just like we did with our suspects for the murders at Pauncefort Hall."

Ruby choked on her gin. "Let's hope that's the only similarity, Feens, let's hope so."

15
———

Lights blazed in the dining room. Fina squinted at the glare from the mirrors placed strategically around the room. Even though it was only 6 o'clock, darkness had descended in the form of pendulous clouds. The doors stood open at either end, creating a welcome cross-breeze in what would otherwise have been suffocating humidity. Despite the impending storm, everyone looked rather cheerful – at least superficially. They were seated at three round tables, set closely enough to one another that guests could converse with those at another table. Nearest the door sat Balraj, Gustave, Phillip, and Ian. They had two empty seats at their table. At the next table sat Captain Mills, Sadie, Emeline and Patricia. Victor and Gilbert were assigned to a small table nearby. Fina instinctively felt this was unnecessary, but noticed they seemed to be having a jolly time creating catapults with peas and their forks. They had been served dinner long before the adults.

"May we sit here?" enquired Ruby, pointing to the two empty chairs.

Phillip Gibbs replied, "Yes, please do. Violet is feeling a touch under the weather, so she's having her dinner brought to her in our cabin. And Gustave just informed us that Miss Dominguez has a headache so she is forgoing dinner all together." Unlike others in formal evening dress, Phillip looked comfortable in his light grey sports jacket. His pipe peeped out of his breast pocket.

Murmuring appropriate sounds of regret and thanks, the pair sat down next to one another. Ruby flounced her silk jersey evening dress in brilliant white as she sat down. Fina also wore silk, though her green dress had flowing skirt panels.

Phillip sat to Fina's left. He slathered butter onto half of a dinner roll, tapped a great deal of salt and pepper on top of the creamy goodness and popped the whole concoction in his mouth. Before he had finished chewing, he prepared the other half of the roll to meet its sister's fate. He tapped his fingers in a jaunty little dance on the tablecloth. He seemed to be completely oblivious to the atmosphere.

Ruby engaged in energetic conversation with Gustave.

"Those designs you showed me were enchanting, Ruby," he said.

Ruby began to wave her hands about. "Thank you, Gustave. Perhaps we could sketch more together before we arrive?"

"Ah, yes, let's see about that. I am rather tired." Then, as if in response to Ruby's crestfallen face, he added, "I'm sure it's just temporary. I expect a good night's sleep will solve that little difficulty."

Fina knew her friend well enough to know that while Ruby could be an enormously dynamic person, the vitality expressed in the conversation with Gustave was forced. Of course, she knew why. Ian was sitting next to Gustave. While he did not stare at Ruby, as Fina thought he might, he did glance at her with a rather sad-puppy look once in a while.

Fina felt conflicted about Ian, but decided that he wasn't

worth her focus at the moment. Something was definitely afoot here, though she couldn't quite get a handle on what.

Her stomach rumbled. Phillip and company had made quick work of the rolls. She glanced at the large clock on the wall. 6:15. Why was it taking so long for the food to be served? She noticed Balraj checking his wristwatch as well, and she gently chided herself for her impatience. Her general level of irritation at mundane events increased with the decrease of food in her stomach.

"You'll have to excuse me," said Balraj as he scraped back his chair. "I feel rather queasy. I think I'd better lie down." Balraj's clipped sentences certainly indicated discomfiture. But it was odd, as he had seemed to be fully engaged in a jovial conversation with Ian a few seconds before.

"Must be the coming storm," said Ian, casually waving away Balraj's exit as well as the smoke from his cigarette.

"Poor chap," said Phillip, chewing on one of the rolls he had hoarded away on his plate. At the next table, laughter suddenly rang out from Sadie, who had been quiet up until then.

Ian continued. "I had a cousin who lived in Istanbul once..."

A piercing shriek interrupted Ian's narrative. It was so high that Fina thought it might crack the glassware.

Everyone jumped in their seats, and all heads turned toward Patricia. "*What* is falling on my head?" she shrieked, shaking her once perfectly coiffed hair as if she were a wet dog. Emeline held up something in her hand with a look of triumph.

"Peas," she pronounced gravely, as if she had discovered a packet of opium on her sister.

Patricia ran her hands carefully through her fine blond hair. "And mashed potatoes – *in my hair*," she said in disgust.

"Who is responsible for this outrage?" said Emeline in a stentorian voice. Really, thought Fina, she would make an excellent barrister.

All eyes turned toward the children's table. The two boys tried to hide their faces.

"It wasn't me, honest, it wasn't me!" cried little Gilbert. "It was him!" retorted Victor, betraying his younger playmate.

"We were trying to pop 'em through the window, the window," said Gilbert, digging himself into a bigger and bigger hole, thought Fina. Gilbert had a nasal, adenoidal voice, so his words tended to tail off into L and M sounds.

Sadie rose from her seat and went over to Victor. "Come, Victor, we need to discuss your behaviour." She nodded at Fina as if to signal she would handle the problem. She patted Victor gently on the back but piloted him rather firmly – despite his protests of innocence – out of the room.

Phillip beckoned Gilbert to come sit up at the table with him in Balraj's vacant chair. He leaned over and whispered into his ear. Gilbert's lower lip stuck out and he crossed his arms in protest. Phillip, having delivered the criticism, then playfully ruffled Gilbert's hair and handed him a glass of water.

When Fina looked up from this scene, she saw that Patricia was gone.

"Where did she go?" she whispered to Ruby.

"She mumbled something about removing mashed potato from her hair, though I think it was actually plantain," she giggled. "Much stickier. Couldn't have happened to a nicer person."

"Ruby!" chided Fina. "So unlike you to be judgmental."

"Well, maybe it's the combination of insufferable hunger, alcohol on an empty stomach and impending seasickness."

"Yes, where is the food? I'm famished."

Ruby sniffed the air. "I think it will arrive soon!"

"You smell it?" asked Fina as she lifted her nose like a piglet tentatively sniffing the air for the first time.

As if on cue, Sarah, Lev and Agnes marched in with enormous silver trays laden with covered ceramic dishes.

Captain Mills leaned over to Ruby. "You're going to love this. Sarah's cooking is almost as good as her poetry. She's prepared conch chowder, cracked conch, stewed fish and souse."

Gustave looked over at them. "I am looking forward to a good meal. This English *cuisine* that you call it in London is most abominable."

"Have you spent much time in England?" asked Fina, less out of interest in the question and more as a diversion from the slowness produced by deliberate ceremony of serving the food.

"I – no, no, not much time. Not much time at all. Just a week or two here and there. As one does," he replied.

And with that inauspicious comment, silence fell on the dining room. Ravenous guests descended on their aromatic, plentiful dishes.

16

———

Fina flung off her thin counterpane – the only bed-clothing left on top of her restless frame. She wiped her moist brow and squinted at the alarm clock on the nightstand. Two in the morning. They had all left the dining room around 7:30. Ian and Gustave had said they were going to the green room for a nightcap before turning in.

The pitching and lurching of the ship had begun to take its toll on both Ruby and Fina, so they had decided that sleep would be a good way to ride out the storm. Fina felt the combination of heavy food, an early bedtime and the sweltering humidity had contributed to her restless sleep. Now she couldn't even call it sleep. It was just restlessness. And a certain... uncertainty.

After dampening herself down in the bathroom, forcing open their small window onto the deck as far as it would go, and returning to bed, she still couldn't sleep. The crashes of the waves and the warbling thunder put her on edge.

She turned over to look at Ruby. As if her friend could sense her gaze, she opened her eyes. Only a bit.

"Are you having trouble sleeping? I am," said Fina with a great sigh of frustration.

Ruby sat upright and turned on the bedside light. She yawned. "Yes, it's been a frightful night so far. And we're not even halfway through it."

Suddenly, her eyes widened. "Did you see that figure moving past our window? They stopped for a minute, and I thought my heart might stop, too!" She pressed a hand to her chest.

Fina twisted her head in the direction of the window. "I didn't see them, but it's probably just Lev, Neville, Sarah or Agnes or even the captain."

"You're right. I don't know why it gave me such a fright. It's perfectly normal for them to be roaming around, especially since they're probably all working through the storm."

"Still," said Fina in a sympathetic tone. "I know what you mean about being on edge."

"You feel it too? I thought it was just my intuition acting up."

Sensing atmosphere accurately was a speciality of Fina's. "No, there's definitely something going on. First of all, it's an eccentric cast of characters on this ship. When pressed, they do seem to have legitimate reasons for being here – at least some of them – but somehow it doesn't add up. They seem so uneasy, and yet I can't say exactly why. It's also odd that so many of them seem to know one another."

"Mmm. Yes. I've wondered about that. Do you think there's someone on board who links them all? There is the Hollywood connection. At least between Dolores and Balraj. And then there's Ian being a producer," Ruby said with a sharp intake of breath.

Letting out the air, she continued. "It is peculiar, and yet, I actually find each story about knowing one another plausible. But you're correct that on the whole, something isn't right."

Fina said, "Since we're obviously not going to be able to sleep, how about a turn on deck?"

As they left the cabin, a sudden lurch of the deck swept Fina's legs out from under her. "Fina!" cried Ruby, clutching her arm as she slid underneath the brass railing outside their cabin door. Fina's legs dangled over the side of the ship, just above the lower deck. She gripped the rail and, with Ruby's assistance, began to pull herself up. Wincing and breathless, she heaved herself onto the deck. There would be many bruises in the morning.

Now upright, Fina bent over, catching her breath.

"Selkies and kelpies, Feens. Are you all right?" Despite herself, Fina gave out a weak laugh at her friend's use of her favourite exclamation.

Wiping her fringe back from her forehead, she said, "I'll be fine. I don't understand how I slipped." As she said this, a huge wave crashed against the boat and they were sent teetering toward their door.

"That's how," said Ruby. "It's quite stormy. Let's go back to our cabin." She retrieved her key from her jacket pocket.

"No, now I'm determined to go for a, well, I suppose I can't call it a stroll."

"More like a roll."

"Exactly. Really – let's try it."

Shrugging her shoulders, Ruby dropped the key back in her pocket and they staggered down the deck. As they turned the corner near the lounge, a great wave crashed against the ship, spraying them with seawater. Now they were as squishy as a bog, thought Fina.

"Let's go downstairs – at least it's covered," said Fina. "It's the one part of the ship Victor and I haven't explored." She was silent about her secret wish that they might run into Neville in the crew's quarters.

They took the stairs slowly, gripping the railings as a small child grips a favourite toy they are asked to share with another child.

At the bottom of the stairs, they stood for a minute, listening to the creaks of the timbers. One door was rhythmically opening and closing with the pitch and roll of the ship.

Fina's stomach rumbled. Why can't you be satisfied for once, she thought. She realised her stomach was more perceptive than her brain. A warm sweet smell wafted through the door.

Both drawn like bears to honey, they tentatively knocked on the swinging door. No answer.

Fina poked her head around the door. She saw a tabby cat lapping up a bowl of cream, even as the bowl tended to slide about the floor. The cat ignored them.

This must be the crew's mess hall. Along one wall hung pots and pans, gently swaying without hitting one another. The other wall was bare, apart from a few pen-and-ink sketches tacked on to the plaster with drawing pins. Fina thought she recognised the style, free-flowing yet confident. Of course – Agnes! She must spend some of her spare time ashore capturing the beautiful Caribbean landscapes.

Down the centre of the room, a long table was covered in a sky-blue cloth. A notebook lay on the table. Looking at the stove, she could see the gas burners were off, but the smell must be coming from the pots on the stove.

Their exploration was interrupted by an "ahem" coming from behind them. Lev.

He smiled and welcomed them to the kitchen with a great circular motion of his arms, as if they were entering his domain. Fina supposed they actually were entering his domain. "Are you hungry? There are some pots with food on the stove."

"Oh no, we couldn't," said Ruby. "We – we were just taking a stroll."

"A stroll? At this time? And in this weather?" Fina noticed something odd about the tone of his voice. His utterances sounded more like statements than questions. He was now standing in front of the table. In front of the notebook.

Feeling that the lack of sleep was finally settling in, Fina and Ruby were silent. Finally gathering her wits, Fina said, "We couldn't sleep. And our cabin was stuffy, so we thought we'd get some fresh air."

Apparently taking her statement at face value or ignoring the implausibility of it, Lev shook his head and said, "Come. I will show you upstairs to your quarters. It is not safe for walking now. You might fall overboard. Or worse."

17

Zzzzzzzzzzz... Fina jolted upright and grabbed the bedclothes. She rubbed her neck where she had felt the mosquito. That incessant buzzing. Now awake, she realised that the sound was not in her head. It was coming from outside the cabin. She must have dreamt the sound was from a mosquito.

Shaking her head, she slid into her silk dressing gown and whispered, "Ruby, wake up."

Ruby peeled open one eye. She shut it again.

"Do you hear that sound? Hmm, it's stopped now. No, there it is again."

Apparently in response, Ruby moved a pillow over her ears.

Fina left her behind to investigate on her own. As she stepped out of the cabin into the bright sunlight, Lev nearly knocked her over as he ran past her.

"What is going on?" she called after him, but he had already turned in the passageway. She made her way down the deck, through the passageway to the left, where she found a small crowd huddled at an open doorway.

Balraj's doorway. Again she heard the sound she had mistaken for a mosquito. It was Agnes, heaving and whining. At regular intervals, she gave a shriek like a fox screaming in the night.

Agnes was rocking back and forth near the doorway.

Trying and failing to peek over Dolores' shoulder, Fina tapped her lightly. "Is Balraj ill?"

Dolores turned. Her eyelids had nearly disappeared into her head. "There's – there's been an accident."

"Ohhh, he's dead, he's dead, dead," yelled Agnes, twisting her apron in her hands.

By this time, it seemed as though the entire ship's crew and passengers had arrived.

"Excuse me, sir, please let me through," said Captain Mills in an officious tone. He gently moved Gustave's arm to the side to wade through the crowd. Fina noticed that Gustave's usually impassive face was still stony – but that his mouth hung open.

From behind her, she felt a light tap on her shoulder. "Feens, what's happened?"

Dolores answered for her. "Balraj is dead."

Ruby held her hand up to the large "O" that was her mouth. "Was he ill?"

With hat tucked underneath his arm, Captain Mills stood in the doorway. "Ahem. May I have your attention, please. I'm afraid there's been an accident. A serious accident. I respectfully request that all guests return to their cabins or partake of the excellent breakfast prepared in the dining room."

A great murmur of excitement and protest erupted from the crowd.

He held up his white-gloved hand. "Please, please, I do require that you accede to my request. It is absolutely necessary."

"What kind of accident was it, Captain?" enquired Emeline – in a tone which implied the captain himself might be the cause of this accident.

"I cannot discuss this matter at this time. As for the crew, I request that you remain until I can discuss further instructions with you." With a little fluttering motion of his hands – as if they were dismissed from class – he disappeared into Balraj's room.

In the dining room, the clink of silverware on plates and the aromas of tea, coffee and eggs would normally provide a pleasant breakfast atmosphere. Usual murmurs about mundane affairs, such as how one slept, or plans for the day were replaced with stolen glances and stares at the horizon outside the windows of the dining room.

For once in her life, Fina's stomach did not respond to the siren call of breakfast. She managed a few bites of dry toast. Ruby's plate, on the other hand, featured a veritable carnival of delectable delights. She could see stewed fish and johnnycakes nestled next to chicken souse.

Distracting herself while Ruby ate, Fina noticed the hunger responses to the tragedy of the other guests. Patricia, hair protected in a fashionable silk wrap, picked at the eggs on her plate – but that was consistent with her general approach to food. She looked gaunt and anxious. Fina noticed that even in her day dress, Patricia wore a large, jewelled brooch. This time it was an iridescent opal dragonfly.

Sadie, too, was not hungry, but that might have been due to Victor's general excitement about events. He was certainly enjoying his breakfast, despite the general pall cast over the room. No, that wasn't quite accurate, thought Fina. The atmosphere wasn't of sadness – everyone's countenances reflected a passivity. Well, she expected that from Gustave, but not from the other passengers. Nervous tension? That wasn't it, either. She had felt that at Pauncefort Hall. It was a kind of restlessness. That was as close as she could get to describing it. She reminded herself to mention it to Ruby later.

"Pass the salt, please, Fina," said Ian as he sat down next to her. He had leaned over and whispered it, as if it were a conspiratorial message he wanted to deliver.

Deciding to play along, she slid the salt toward him and whispered, "Do you know what happened? You're friends with the captain, so maybe he told you something."

Ian dabbed his corners of his mouth, then set his arms on the table. He lowered his voice to such a volume that Fina felt she had to become a lip-reader. "It looks as though Balraj must have been murdered. He died from a blow to the back of his head. I suppose it could have been an accident, but it seems unlikely."

Fina involuntarily gripped his arm. He winced. She removed it immediately after realising her nails had grown quite long. "But how do you know it's not an accident – maybe he was knocked over by a wave and hit his head in the storm?"

Nodding, he said, "Yes, I agree that is plausible, but there's just one problem. He was right inside the cabin, and there's no evidence of anything having come into contact with his head."

"Perhaps he wandered into his cabin after being hurt outside on deck."

"It's a good thought, but the blow was quite severe. I doubt he could have made it more than a few steps without falling down. Besides, he'd have to open the cabin door – most likely with a key, unless he left it unlocked."

"What are you two whispering about?" enquired Ruby while she delicately wiped her mouth. "Let me guess," she said with a slow smile.

Darting a glance around the room and the morose crowd, Ian responded, "Let's move out on deck."

"Good idea," said Fina. "We don't want to disturb the murderer's breakfast."

Fina was following him out when she felt Ruby grab her arm, pulling her back into the dining room.

"We can't trust Ian," Ruby murmured in her ear. "I know he's charming – you know how charming I think he is – but he is up to something and we still don't know what."

Fina felt hurt that Ruby could think her naive, but she nodded nonetheless. She knew that Ruby's complex relationship with Ian made her more cautious.

Placing her hand on Ruby's upper arm, she said, "I know, I know. But this murder might be our chance to find our contact. Let's play along with Ian to see where it gets us."

The smile of relief on Ruby's face signalled she was right.

Out on deck, Ian's eyebrows wiggled in amusement.

"Why are you smiling, Ian? Murder is hardly worthy of a laugh," said Fina.

"'Disturb the murderer's breakfast!' I forgot how blunt you are, Fina. It is an endearing trait," he said as he brushed an invisible piece of lint from his blazer sleeve.

"Condescension is hardly flattering, Ian," said Ruby with a look of real venom in her eyes.

Taking a long drag on his cigarette, Ian's eyes crinkled in amusement. "Touché, dear Ruby. You're right. As usual."

Tapping her foot, Ruby said, "Well? What do you want of us? Are you here to interrogate us?"

"Ah, well, no. You see, this murder has made matters, well, more complicated. Maxwell – the captain, that is – and I go way back. He's asked me to look into the matter for him. Keep things... discreet, you know," he said with a wink.

"No, we don't know," Ruby huffed. "I'm certainly no fan of the police, but why wouldn't we travel to the nearest island to alert the so-called authorities?"

The captain sidled up to Ian. His bearing was as military as ever, though there was an added stiffness, no doubt due to the stress of the tragedy.

Looking toward Ian, he cleared his throat. "As I'm sure

Ian's told you, we need to find out who caused this tragedy as soon as possible. Unfortunately, we had to veer off course because of the storm last night. That means we could travel due west to a number of islands, but at this point it would take just as long to do that as it would to go directly to Port of Spain. We are in the Atlantic more than the Caribbean at this point."

"Go on," said Ruby.

"So given your superior sleuthing skills that Ian told me about, I was hoping the two of you could join Ian in investigating this murder. We'd like to clear it up before we arrive. I know you two will understand why."

Ruby looked at Fina. Fina nodded.

"We'll see what we can do, Captain Mills. Thank you for your trust in us," said Ruby.

With a grin of thanks, he spun round on his shiny shoes and marched down the deck.

Turning her gaze back to Ian, Ruby said, "Assuming we say yes – or I should say yes to working with you – can you guarantee that our sleuthing won't come back to haunt us when we arrive in Port of Spain? And that you'll keep our other *activities* at Pauncefort a secret?"

Placing his hand over his heart and giving a little bow, Ian said, "You have my word, dear ladies."

"Well, we agree. Let's get started." Ruby and Fina moved to walk toward the scene of the crime.

"Wait," said Ian. "You two aren't on any sort of other business on this trip?"

Ruby stopped abruptly and turned. Her full skirt swished back like a cross-cutting wave. She drew close to Ian. Very close. So close Fina could barely hear her.

"Let's be quite clear. We agree to help you, but you do not get to interrogate us. I am travelling to Port of Spain as Gustave's assistant. Fina is here as a governess. That is all. Now, any more questions?"

Ian shook his lowered head, eyebrows furrowed.

Turning back again, Ruby marched down the deck, head held high.

18

―――

Tremendous waves of nausea washed over Fina. Scampering out of Balraj's cabin to the fresh air on deck, she leaned over the hot metal railing. Blessed relief rushed through her as the need to retch passed. Viewing dead bodies was not a new experience – she had seen her own father dead, as well as those who had been killed at Pauncefort Hall – but that *blood*. It wasn't the quantity of blood, as there was precious little of it. No, she turned queasy when she saw the sticky, matted patch of blood on the back of the crushed skull.

Mustn't think about it, she repeated to herself. Her mind wandered to a pleasant image of the lush green woods near their house in Tavistock. The memories of her father's death and brother's execution rose up from the recesses of her brain. Focus on the forest, Fina. Focus. This new technique helped with her worry and tension, especially when those searing memories emerged from the depths of her subconscious.

Fina relaxed her taut eyelids and gazed at the azure horizon. As she sucked in the sea air, the tempest in her stomach began to subside. Determined to be strong, she spun on her heel and marched back into the dreaded cabin.

Balraj's body now lay beneath a generously sized white sheet. Fina gave Ian a grateful grimace. She decided that being useful would be a good cover to her embarrassment. What better way to be useful than to become the official scribe? She pulled out the small notebook from her clutch and perched on the edge of the bed. Her pen poised itself above the notebook, ready for the start of a race.

Ruby nodded at Fina and began her commentary. "It seems definite that Balraj was killed by a blow to his head. Of course, he could have been killed some other way that doesn't show trauma – such as poison – but there are no obvious signs of that."

"I agree," said Ian. "But where's the murder weapon?"

Ruby tapped her teeth. "Good question. Nothing seems obvious," she said as she scanned the room.

"I suppose the murderer could have chucked whatever it was overboard," said Fina.

Ruby sighed in return. "That does seem the most plausible option. Why hold onto it?"

Ian nodded in agreement. "So he was hit near the top of his skull, not at the back of his head. Balraj was short – I'd say only a bit taller than Fina."

Fina gave Ian a glare of mock offence.

"So that means the attacker was taller than him, or maybe similar height?" enquired Fina.

"Yes, that's plausible," said Ruby. "I suppose a shorter person could have lifted the weapon high above their head, but they'd need a great deal of strength."

"The upshot is that we're looking for a relatively tall murderer," said Ian. "Though we cannot rule anyone out for certain at this stage," he said as a hasty rejoinder.

"I'll make a list," said Fina, turning a page to start a new sheet.

"That would be Sadie, Phillip and Emeline," said Ian.

"And you, Ian," said Ruby with a smile.

Sighing, he nodded his head. "And you, dear Ruby. I'd gander you were perhaps five-foot seven?"

Now it was her turn to sigh and nod. "As for the crew, I'd say Sarah, Maxwell and Neville are all tall enough. Agnes and Lev are quite short."

Fina had been scribbling furiously, but her pen suddenly scratched to a halt.

Ruby glanced up. "Are you thinking what I'm thinking, Fina?"

"I think so. Heels."

Ruby nodded sagely.

"Heels?" enquired Ian.

"Yes, we shouldn't rule out guests using high-heeled shoes in order to get a bit of height. That might elevate them enough to hit poor Balraj on the head."

"So that means we need to include Patricia, Violet, Dolores, and Agnes," he said with a sigh.

"And Lev and Gustave as well," said Ruby, quietly.

Ian's eyebrows wiggled again. "I don't understand. Do you mean...?"

Ruby rolled her eyes. It was a rare occurrence, so Fina savoured it. "You work in the theatre, Ian. Use your imagination – not to mention your experience."

"I suppose, but what if they were caught?" said Ian, wiping his brow with a handkerchief.

"They could slip them off and on. Besides, if I were the murderer, I'd be much more worried about being seen at all. A non-conforming wardrobe would be the least of my worries," said Ruby.

"Do you think a woman could have done it? I mean, would she be strong enough?" asked Ian.

"Good Lord, Ian," said Fina. "Your views on gender are positively archaic."

Ian shot back, "Hardly, dear Fina. They may be archaic in your small social circles."

Ruby was lively as a fire. She added, "And another point! The very idea that gender exists..." She stopped herself.

Ian grinned. "I may be archaic, but at least I am open. Point taken," he said with a little curtsy to them both.

Fina's nose began to twitch. What was that scent? She had thought she smelt it earlier, but had assumed it was in her head. "Do you two smell that? It smells faintly of perfume. Did Balraj wear cologne?"

"Not that I'm aware of," said Ian. "Perhaps light aftershave, I suppose, but I cannot remember smelling it. Can you, Ruby?"

Ruby shook her head. "No, but my nose cannot be trusted. Fina has a very developed sense of smell. Let's figure out where it is coming from."

Motioning to Fina, the two approached the writing desk. The surface held a gold wristwatch, a small travel clock, a few pens and paper, along with a small assortment of bottles. Fina held each bottle to her nose, wagging her finger each time to indicate a negative result.

"Let's try the bathroom," said Fina.

"Good idea," said Ian. "We haven't looked in there yet."

The three of them squeezed into the tiny bathroom. Nothing unusual met the eye, thought Fina. Toothbrush, tooth powder, comb, razor and soap. Fina held up the rather luxurious pomade jar and green *mal de mer* tonic bottle. Nothing.

As they re-entered the bedroom, Ruby dropped down on her haunches to move closer to the floor. "Look at the rug." Fina and Ian followed suit.

As if instructing her pupils in the fine art of rug excavation, Ruby spread her hand out in a grand gesture. "Do you see how the patterned rug looks slightly discoloured? At first I thought it was a stain," she said, gently touching the pattern. "But now I realise it is the result of the rug material – what would you call it?"

"Isn't it the nap of the rug?" said Ian, helpfully.

"Aren't you a fount of knowledge," said Ruby. "Yes. See where the nap is raised? It means that unless Balraj brushed up against the rug himself, or moved the furniture, something else was dragged across here."

Ian's eyes grew wide. "Such as a body?"

"Selkies and kelpies!" said Fina, duly impressed by her friend's brainpower.

"So why drag the body?" asked Ian, moving his legs around as he stood up.

Following suit, Ruby said, "Yes, exactly. Why?"

She frowned.

"What is it?" asked Ian.

"Well, it's a shame that the entire floor isn't covered in rugs. We cannot tell if the murderer dragged the body from some-where else in the room, or even from outside the cabin," said Ruby.

"Yes, it is a shame—" Ian stopped himself, mid-sentence. He held his finger up in a rather theatrical gesture. That was to be expected, Fina reminded herself.

He bent down over the body and made a motion to pull back the sheet. He paused. "Fina, you might want to look away for a moment."

"Gladly," she said, turning her head.

"I knew there was something strange about the body," said Ruby. "You're brilliant, Ian!"

Fina wished she could have seen the look on Ian's face when Ruby called him brilliant. Her stomach gave a little flip of happi-ness – perhaps mixed with a teensy bit of jealousy.

"May I look now?" asked Fina.

"Yes, Feens," said Ruby. "Ian realised that there was no blood, or ahem..."

"Grey cell matter," interjected Ian.

"Disgusting!" said Fina.

"I agree," said Ian. "But nevertheless there is little evidence of the murder actually occurring right here." He pointed at the rug.

"What's even more peculiar is the absence of blood on the rug, where the body had been dragged," said Ruby.

"I'd better write these points down so we don't forget them," said Fina, rushing over to her notebook.

Engrossed in the rug, Ian continued. "Is it possible that the murderer just tidied up after themselves?"

Ruby gave a half nod, smoothing her dress and hair. "I suppose that's possible. But it would take a lot of trouble: they'd have to have cleaning supplies, and nerves of steel, and a very good reason. Why? Why commit a murder and then clean up after it? What were they trying to hide?"

19

Fina guzzled her iced tea. She held the glass to her cheek. It was a hot day already and the mercury was rising by the minute.

Ian, Ruby, and Fina had decided to divvy up their tasks. Ruby and Fina would interview as many guests as possible while Ian would talk to the captain about what they had found so far. Thus, they found themselves in Dolores' room – a natural place for them to start. The room looked different than their own, even though all the cabins had the same design and knick-knacks. Dolores had rearranged the furniture so the bedroom felt more like a sitting room.

After exchanging niceties about Ruby's sketches, they settled down to the matter that was on everyone's minds.

"I understand you and Balraj were quite close," said Ruby.

Dolores' hands flew up to her delicate features. She touched her temple and began to rub it, rhythmically. "I wouldn't say close. We knew each other, of course, as we were both actors – and faced the same types of discrimination. But, I'd say our friendship was based on our careers rather than things we really had in common."

"Was Balraj giving you career advice the other day in the

lounge?" enquired Fina.

Dolores shifted in her seat. "I don't know what you're talking about."

Ruby reached over to Dolores and touched her lightly on the arm. "We understand you must be very upset, Dolores," said Ruby. "But we're just trying to find out what happened."

Sitting back in the chair, Dolores responded, "I know. I want to find out what happened too – but I don't know why I should trust you. You see, for most of my life, the people I've trusted have let me down. And with murder, well, I don't have to tell you," she said, looking directly at Ruby. "Let's just say I want to play it safe. It's not as if I can ask for my attorney to be present."

"Maybe we could start off, instead, with what you know about what happened last night," said Fina.

A gentle breeze floated in through the door, ruffling Dolores' hair. She reached up to pat it back into place. She was clearly unconvinced.

"I'm happy to answer that question for you, but I don't really understand why you and Ruby have apparently been deputised as detectives."

Ruby glanced at Fina. "You see, we're friends with Ian and Ian is friends with the captain. About five months ago when we first met Ian – at an ill-fated weekend party in England – there was a similar type of incident. Fina and I had the good fortune to be able to solve that particular mystery. That's why Ian asked us to essentially become part of the investigation – especially because there are no police anywhere in sight. He trusts us and the captain trusts Ian."

Dolores nodded her head slowly, as if the information needed a little time to sink in. "I think I'm beginning to see what you mean. Are you saying it's better that we investigate this now, rather than wait for the so-called authorities when we arrive in Port of Spain?"

"Exactly," said Ruby.

"All right, I guess I'll play along. What do you want to know about last night?"

Feeling that the time was right to pull out her notebook, Fina prepared for some furious scribbling. This was the one and only time she wished she had learned shorthand.

"When did you retire to your cabin with a headache?" Ruby queried.

"About 6 o'clock that evening. I had had a bite to eat in the green room – I thought it would make me feel better – but it didn't. I came back to my cabin, took a cold shower, and then went to bed."

"When do you think you actually drifted off to sleep?" asked Fina.

"I think it must've been about 6:15, but I couldn't be sure. I do take sleeping pills, and they usually knock me out right away."

Dolores stared at the ceiling, eyes moving back and forth rapidly as if they were a typewriter carriage. "I woke up during the night. Looking back, I think it was because of some sort of noise. It was coming from the direction of Balraj's cabin."

"What kind of noise was it?" asked Ruby.

"That's the trouble. You know how you wake up because of a noise, but you don't really hear the actual sound – because you were asleep? That's what happened."

"What time was it you heard the noise?" asked Fina, not looking up from her scribbling.

Dolores sighed. "It was all over so quickly – I awoke, listened for a minute and then drifted back to sleep. I didn't look at the clock. I do have a fairly well developed internal clock, however, so my guess is that it was maybe one or two in the morning – though that is a shot in the dark, as they say."

"Did you hear anything else?" asked Ruby.

"No, wait," Dolores stopped and cocked her head to one side

as if listening carefully to herself. "I do remember a loud knocking noise. It must've been about 6:45 because I remember looking at my clock."

"Was it coming from Balraj's cabin?" enquired Ruby. "Or was it the direction of Gustave's cabin?"

"I was already groggy, but I'm fairly certain it came from Balraj's direction. Though I couldn't tell if the knocking was on the outside of the door or on the inside of the door."

Ruby jumped up. "Well, there's one way to find out."

Their experiment confirmed that Dolores had indeed heard the door knocking from outside the cabin rather than inside.

Alone once more, Ruby and Fina stood on deck, debating the next suspect to interview.

"Hmm. I think we should talk to Gustave next," said Ruby. "After all, I have a connection with him so we may get more information than we will from other passengers."

"I think we should speak to Violet, too. Even though she was in her cabin, she might have heard something," said Fina.

Then a sudden rush of guilty adrenaline coursed through her limbs. Victor! How could she forget? "Where's my head? I should be looking after Victor. In the upheaval of everything that's happened, I completely forgot about my duties. Sadie will be quite peeved."

"You know you shouldn't feel poorly about it. We've both experienced death before, but it's still a shock. Everyone is in shock. In fact, I'm sure the murderer is in shock as well – perhaps a shock of a different kind. Be good to yourself, Feens."

Fina's shoulders relaxed. "Yes, you're right. I just had that feeling you get when you notice something's missing. In my case, a little red-headed, bespectacled something."

Ruby tapped her teeth. A sure sign her brain was engaged. "Something missing. Yes, that's interesting."

Had she had a breakthrough? Fina waited in suspense.

"Or perhaps something that's *not* missing," Ruby mused. Tap, tap.

No more was forthcoming. Shaking her head as if to return to reality, Ruby said, "Let's go together to talk to Sadie. In the meantime, I'll let this little idea of mine – yours, actually – marinate."

Knowing better than to press for more information when Ruby's ideas needed time to percolate, Fina smiled and stayed silent.

As they strode through the passageway, a ruckus erupted from the direction of Patricia and Emeline's cabin. Fina motioned to Ruby to listen. They crept up opposite the door. Fina removed a small pair of field glasses from her bag.

"Just in case they come out – we can look as though we're whale watching," whispered Fina.

"Brilliant!" Ruby whispered back.

The crash of the sea against the ship made the whole listening business as choppy as the waves, thought Fina.

"Now that he's dead, that stream of money to his ghastly causes will stop." Fina could just make out Emeline's voice.

"I could care less about those damn causes, Emmy. But that money that was funding his pet projects was affecting the price of our oil shares. Now those disturbances to the market should stop – within a few months. Crisis will be averted," Patricia answered.

"Well, that means that you can reinstate my allowance. You know how much money I need for the eugenics work. It is a cause of the highest moral and scientific order. It's—"

"Oh, go stuff your moral and scientific order. Not a penny more, do you understand, Emmy. Not a penny more!"

Crash. It sounded like a lamp might have fallen on the floor. Crikey.

Fina's and Ruby's heads turned simultaneously to one another. Ruby's eyes widened.

Heavy footsteps – like a goose-stepping general – approached the door. Fina and Ruby scrambled around the corner.

Slam. Quickly, Ruby and Fina changed their postures, indicating they were just casually strolling down the passageway.

Emeline whipped around the corner, leaning at an angle like a charging bull. Her hair, usually pulled back in a clenched bun, had fallen to the side. Wisps of hair fell around her face like cobwebs. Her wool turtleneck looked as if it were ready to strangle her already strained throat. She held a briefcase. It slipped through her fingers to the floor. As she retrieved it, slips of paper escaped, fluttering about in the gentle sea breeze.

She shrieked. "Please, please help me retrieve these papers," she said as she ran to scoop up the closest escapee. Ruby and Fina set to work and soon returned the sheaf of typewritten pages. Fina glanced at what was clearly a title page. It read "No Escape". Must be one of her frightful eugenics or marriage promotion screeds, she thought.

As she tucked one of the loose strands of hair behind her ear, Emeline said, "I'm most grateful to you two." She hugged the papers to her chest. Fina couldn't help but admire her self-command. It must have cost her some considerable effort to bite back her pride and accept help from someone who had slapped her face only the day before, but she managed it with aplomb. Perhaps she was used to fielding violent opposition to her views.

Sensing a grand opportunity, Fina took the lead. "Glad to be of service, Miss Caulk. I know we're all feeling at loose ends after what happened this morning."

"Yes, it is such a tragedy. But I always say that you shall reap what you sow. And really, what can you expect from…"

It took all of Fina's strength not to look in Ruby's direction.

She could only imagine her facial expression. Anger rose up in her – again – but she knew she had to play nice.

Deciding the best course was to ignore Emeline's insults, Fina said, "We've been trying to piece together what happened last night. Did you see Balraj – that is, before you went to bed?"

Regaining her composure, Emeline began to reshuffle the sheaf of papers into a neat rectangle. "No, I did not. I know one should not speak ill of the dead—"

But you're going to do it anyway, thought Fina. She gently held Ruby's arm, as much to restrain herself as Ruby.

Emeline continued, "But really, I do my best to steer clear of such *men.*"

"Quite, Miss Caulk. What time did you happen to go to bed?"

"Well, I couldn't sleep. I suppose it was the combination of going to bed early, the frightful temperature, and the storm. So I took my travel typewriter and went to the lounge. I need to complete a pamphlet before we arrive."

"What time did you go to the lounge and when did you finally go to bed?" asked Fina.

"I'm not quite sure what time I went to the lounge – it must've been near 11 o'clock. I do remember looking at the clock when I left, which must've been around 2 in the morning."

"And your sister?"

"She was asleep when I left our cabin at 11 o'clock. You'll have to ask her yourself to see if she left between 11 and 2." Emeline had now reinserted the papers into her briefcase and she made motions to leave. "And now, I must leave you two to work on my new book."

"Just one more thing, Miss Caulk," said Fina. "Who do you think killed Balraj?"

"I should think that's perfectly obvious. It must be that steward – Mr Raymond."

20

———

"Good Lord," exclaimed Ruby after Emeline had scuttled away. "That woman's behaviour is horrid. I'm glad you took the lead on that interview," she said as she let out a long stream of air.

"It took all my strength – as I know it did yours – not to slap her again into consciousness," Fina said. She hesitated. "You don't think there's anything in her accusation, do you?"

"I don't think we can eliminate anyone from the suspect list, but I cannot fathom any motive for Neville. Besides, Emeline didn't offer any evidence, so I'm sure we can chalk it up to her, ah, beliefs. I cannot call them principles because they are inherently unprincipled."

Feeling ashamed that she had even entertained the idea – especially? – about Neville, Fina changed the subject by knocking on Sadie's cabin door.

Creak.

Sadie's head popped out through a tiny crack of the doorway. Fina couldn't understand how Sadie's head could fit through such a small opening. Her eyes were red and glazed with the telltale film of already-cried tears.

"Oh, it's you. You'd better come in. Please do join us, Miss

Dove," Sadie said, opening the door a tad further – as if she were afraid some interloper might pop in behind them.

As they entered, Sadie shifted magazines, clothes and other various and sundry items from two chairs. "I'm sorry about the mess. I could blame it on Victor," she said, ruffling the child's hair as he kept his nose in his book. "But that wouldn't be fair. I'm torn up about this murder," she said, nearly falling into the soft covers of the bed. Her arms flopped by her side like a rag doll's, giving the impression she had been dropped from a great height.

Seizing the opportunity, Ruby said, "Lady Winchcombe-Twisleton—"

"Please, call me Sadie."

"Yes. Sadie. We've all been upset by this murder. Fina and I have been informally speaking to other passengers to see if we can find out what occurred."

Sadie's chin shot up abruptly. "Shouldn't we leave that to the police?"

"The captain has informed us that we've veered off course – due to the storm. It will take just as much time for us to sail to Port of Spain as it would to any other island. He'll involve the authorities after we've arrived. But that's still two days away," said Ruby.

"So you're—"

"We're just doing the best we can to find out what happened. Did you know Balraj well?"

"Why do you think I knew Balraj?"

"I did see you have that exchange with him on the first night," interjected Fina.

Sadie's eyes narrowed. She licked her lips. "I see you two have been talking."

Feeling defensive, Fina scrambled to reply, but was lost for words. Balraj had been so over-familiar and patronising, even in his brief interaction with Sadie, that it was impossible to question her about it without repeating the insult. Luckily, Ruby intervened, and Fina felt her muscles relax.

"We were just discussing who knew Balraj before the voyage – so we could find out more about his character," said Ruby.

"Well, I cannot say that I was a fan of Balraj. He was, let's say, opportunistic. I first met him at some sort of theatre party in the West End perhaps a year ago. I've seen him occasionally at social events. We were acquaintances more than anything else," said Sadie.

She took one of her omnipresent compacts from the side table and began to powder her nose, clearly signalling this line of questioning was to halt.

Fina decided it was wise not to press her further. They had to find out why she was so upset with him. The reaction she'd had that evening, and his extraordinary manner, certainly suggested they were more than mere acquaintances. Perhaps they'd had a secret affair?

Ruby apparently agreed with Fina's decision, as she changed course. "Do you remember what time you left the dining room with Victor last night?"

She snapped the compact shut. "You can't think, you can't think I had anything to do with—" she paused, looked at Victor and cupped one hand near her mouth to whisper, "A murder?"

Fina replied, "No, Sadie, we're just trying to establish where everyone was during and after dinner."

Clearly forgetting the dangerous implications of this drama, Sadie warmed to the subject with a conspiratorial air. "Well, I believe we left at 6:20 – because I did look at the clock. That Burbage woman left at about the same time. You should look into her background, I think. She's all wrapped up in investments and philanthropy. Augustus – that's my late husband,

Lord Winchcombe-Twisleton – mentioned Burbage Oil a few times at some charitable events balls."

"Did he talk about his causes with you often?" asked Fina, hoping that the question didn't seem odd to Sadie.

"Oh no, Auggie and I never talked about his business or his charitable causes. But I remember it because it came up in our conversations with others over cocktails," she sighed. "He was immensely proud of all the money he raised. He received a number of awards for his work to cure a rare toenail fungal growth, you know. A stupendous achievement."

Fina avoided looking at Ruby, knowing full well that the burbling giggle in her chest would escape if she glanced in her direction.

"Why does the Burbage Oil connection matter for the murder?" asked Ruby with a face so straight Fina knew it was the result of enormous effort.

"Ah, I just think that Mrs Burbage has her hand in many different... affairs," said Sadie.

Ruby shot Fina an almost imperceptible glance. File that away for later, thought Fina.

"Victor fell asleep around 8 and I drifted off maybe an hour later. We slept soundly – or at least I did."

Peering down at her son, Sadie said, "Victor, honey, did you wake up at all last night?" Victor did not look up from his reading. Fina felt relieved that he hadn't been listening to their conversation. Sadie repeated her question.

"No, Mama, but I did have bad dreams. A big spider was crawling and she caught me in her web. I was so scared," he said, putting his little hand on her knee. She returned the gesture and gave him a reassuring squeeze.

Interview over, they left the cabin. "All this questioning has given me an appetite," said Fina.

Ruby smiled fondly at her. "Now why does that not surprise

me? In any case, I heard the lunch gong sound a few minutes ago."

But their progress toward the dining hall was interrupted by a tall figure. Patricia. There was no avoiding her as she bore down on them.

"Miss Dove." Patricia spoke in a stage whisper that was clearly audible all along the deck. "In the wake of recent events, I must enquire whether you have had any success in identifying the miscreant who planted that poisonous beast in my bed."

"Mrs Burbage," said Ruby, assuming a similarly formal manner. "As I said to you yesterday, Fina and I are not undertaking any private commissions while we are on board this ship. I am sorry to disappoint, but in view of the fact that there has been a murder, we must focus our energy on that for the time being."

Even Patricia could hardly argue with that. Fina was pleased to see her speechless for a moment. But she soon rallied.

"Well! I should have thought it was obvious to anyone that I myself was the intended victim of this particular crime." She paused, clearly expecting a reaction.

As none was forthcoming, she continued.

"Even though the threats against me are intensifying by the day, I can see that I shall have to take matters into my own hands. As it happens, I have an excellent strategy for identifying the perpetrator. And since I am not inclined to take you into my confidence, you shall have to wait and see how my plan unfolds."

With that, she swept off in the direction of the dining hall. Ruby and Fina gazed after her.

"Selkies and kelpies! I wonder what devilment she's got up her sleeve," mused Fina.

"The devil only knows."

21

A gurgling sound arose from the depths of Fina's stomach. She watched with pleasant anticipation as Sarah, Agnes, and Lev weaved their way through the maze of tables in the dining room. Both doors were open, letting in a cool cross breeze that seemed to invigorate conversations from a lull to a low rumble.

Gustave sat patiently next to her at a small table in a corner. He had agreed to lunch with Ruby and Fina – to discuss the events of the night before. Though he objected at first – on gastronomical grounds of mixing sordid conversation with the sacred act of eating a meal – he soon realised that it was to his advantage to tell all he knew as soon as possible.

As she munched on a piece of bread, Fina contemplated Gustave. With his affable manner, which induced people to open up to him, he might turn out to be quite a useful ally, she thought. Natty as always, he wore a chocolate linen suit with the burgundy handkerchief square in the pocket. His hands moved rapidly – they were certainly more expressive than his face – making sweeping gestures while he spoke to Ruby.

After finishing her bread with a satisfying gulp, Fina asked,

"Gustave, what did you do before you were a designer? You had a career before this, correct?"

He looked down in his lap and brushed away some crumbs before answering. "Ah, yes. A bit of this and that. Office work, mostly."

Ruby shifted in her chair, giving Fina the signal that the real questioning should begin. They'd better hurry before Sarah made her way to the table.

Gustave pre-empted their questions with a succinct report. "As for this crime, you know we all left the dining room together. I went with Ian to have a nightcap and then went to bed, perhaps thirty minutes later. I read the newest Simenon mystery and fell asleep not long after that."

Ruby asked, "Did you hear anything during the night or wake up at all and hear anything?"

"Surely you do not believe Balraj died during the night?" He smiled. "You two are not the only detectives on the ship! I, too, have been doing – how do you say? – a bit of sleuthing. I asked Miss Gidge when she left the tray of food for Balraj. She said she knocked and knocked at 6:45 but there was no answer. She decided to leave the tray – even though it was stormy – because the food would get cold in any case. When she came this morning to pick up the tray, it was still there untouched, though she thought it had been moved."

"Moved?" said Fina. "The boat was rocking last night – perhaps it just slid on the deck."

Gustave nodded in an approving manner. "Correct, Miss Aubrey Havelock. That must've been the case."

"And do you have any theories about why someone would want to kill Balraj?"

He scratched the side of his head tentatively and then moved both hands to his lap. "No. Balraj was a delightful, if somewhat dramatic personage. I enjoyed his company immensely and he was a very generous person. He was always ready to snatch an opportunity."

That was the second time someone mentioned his opportunistic character, thought Fina.

Ruby stiffened, almost imperceptibly. She said in a forced-casual voice, "What kind of opportunity?"

"What I mean is, he'd snatch an opportunity if it came to him, but he lived by a specific code of principles. While people may not have agreed with his principles, he lived by them and therefore had integrity." Gustave's fluting voice held an unusual note of respect.

As if by magic, a steaming plate of food appeared before Fina. She looked up gratefully at Sarah, who was busy setting down Ruby's and Gustave's dishes. She scanned the room quickly to see if everyone else had been served. Perhaps they could ask Sarah to sit for a minute.

"Thank you for this scrumptious-looking food, Miss Breeze!" she said with enthusiasm. She snapped her napkin with a flourish before smoothing it on her lap.

"Miss Breeze, would you have a very quick moment to sit with us?" asked Ruby. "I'd like to ask you something."

Sarah looked around. "I should be getting back to my kitchen," she said, pausing and thinking. "But I suppose one moment won't hurt."

She sat down, tentatively, almost hovering above her chair. "What would you like to know, Miss Dove?"

"We heard that Miss Gidge left a tray of food for Mr Chadha at 6:45 and did not return to pick it up until the next morning – when she found the food was untouched, and then discovered the body."

Sarah shook her head, sadly. "A real tragedy. He was a kind man. He treated me well. You're right about Agnes. She said it was 6:45. She also brought trays down to Miss Dominguez and

Mrs Gibbs at about 6. They both opened the door to take their trays – so we know they were both in their cabins. I assume that's what you're after," she said with a slow, shrewd smile.

Ruby returned the smile. "Absolutely. Do you have any theories about who might have murdered Mr Chadha?"

"I've hardly had time out of my kitchen. But I have heard odd goings-on here. Odd indeed."

Clink, clink, clink. Fina turned around to see who had called for a toast.

Patricia rose slowly, looking quite regal in her printed leaf-pattern dress with a sailor-style cravat, all pinned together with a large silver owl brooch.

"Ahem. Given the rather ghastly events on this ship," she said, voice rising in a crescendo, "I propose we endeavour to contact Mr Chadha directly."

Silence.

So that was what she had been planning. The woman must have lost her marbles. All that money must have made her brain soft, thought Fina.

Patricia pulled out a white, almost heart-shaped disc from her bag, just like a magician. She held it aloft and slowly rotated it around the room so everyone could see.

Violet squeaked, "A Ouija board!"

Patricia nodded, bestowing a look of sisterhood upon Violet. "Yes, I propose we contact Balraj directly via séance."

A general murmur of shock or approval – it was impossible to tell which – went up among the now-satiated passengers. Perhaps it was approval since everyone must be in a better mood after all that delicious food.

Fina rolled her eyes at Ruby. As she looked at her friend, however, she saw her face was less sceptical than she'd imagined it would be.

Patricia took the murmuring crowd to be a sign of approval.

She began to pull the curtains around the dining room, thus blocking out the powerful light of the midday sun. Lev and Sarah pulled together a few tables to create a large circle-like arrangement with chairs for everyone.

The effect was hardly atmospheric. The thin curtains filtered rather than blocked the sun, producing twilight rather than darkness. Nonetheless, everyone seemed to be taking the task rather seriously. Soon they were all seated around the large circle.

"I would like you all to please place your hands lightly on this planchette," Patricia said. "There is no need to exert any pressure; the spirit force will provide. Then could you all please close your eyes. And keep them closed," she added pointedly.

Gustave's hand shook as he put his fingertips on the planchette. Sadie knocked over a glass of water, causing a minor disturbance. Phillip had to sneeze, so he broke the chain of clasped hands, delaying the event even further.

Finally, once they had all settled down, the only noise Fina could hear was Gilbert and Victor softly mimicking animal calls as they played with their toys in the far corner of the dining room.

Patricia inhaled deeply and then exhaled with a slight wheeze. Must be the cigarettes, thought Fina. She fluttered her hands over the board with surprising gentleness. All eyes were fixed on the planchette as it trembled lightly under the pressure of their fingertips. Patricia motioned to them all to close their eyes.

"Is there anybody there?" Patricia intoned, lowering her voice at least two octaves.

The planchette quivered.

"Are you there, Balraj?" asked Patricia.

The white disc moved slowly, spelling Y-E-S. The stillness in the room was absolute.

"Balraj, can you speak to us?"

Again the planchette drifted to the Y, but then paused, hovering, as if reluctant to continue.

Selkies and kelpies, thought Fina. This is rubbish.

Patricia's voice seemed to go even lower, if that were possible. "You have crossed over to the Other Side. We need to know about your death, if we are to protect the living." Was that a note of fear in her voice? "Balraj, please tell us... was your death an accident?"

The planchette gave a sudden leap and skittered about on the Ouija board.

Patricia took a deep breath. "Balraj... *there must be no more tragedies.* You must tell us: who is the murderer?"

Fina detected a definite shift in collective body language. It was as if everyone's body slowly stiffened.

A breeze ruffled a curtain drawn over an open window.

Fina opened her eyes – just a crack – to see everyone's faces. Ruby's fluttering eyelids indicated that she was doing the same. So was Ian.

Patricia repeated her question, but the planchette stayed put. She shifted in her seat, eyes still closed.

"Why were you murdered, Balraj?"

Now the planchette skidded across the board, gaining speed. It went to the M, then the O.

As the planchette danced about, Fina's barely opened eyes scanned everyone's faces. To her dismay, she saw that Patricia was also peeking out from under her half-closed eyelids. Fina hastily squinched her eyes shut to avoid being caught. Patricia's haughty voice intoned the rest of the planchette's message. "N... E... Y."

At that, Fina opened her eyes completely. Patricia's face was contorted in an expression of utter surprise. Whose face had she seen?

22

A warm sun bathe on the deck was just what Fina needed. She tensed and relaxed her muscles, tossing her arms over the arms of the lounge chair. Turning on her side, she looked at Ruby in the adjacent chair. Looking glamorous as always, she had on round sunglasses and an emerald green swimming costume. She was reading the Makhno book, this time more carefully than before.

Although lunch's séance offered tasty food for thought, they had both turned sluggish due to a natural lull in energy and a hearty meal. Instead of fighting it, Ruby suggested they position themselves on the sundeck in such a way that they might be able to overhear conversations. Conversations about m-o-n-e-y.

Not forgetting their primary task of making contact, either, Ruby thought it a good way to be available for someone to approach them. Fina felt fortunate that Sadie had said she did not need to give Victor lessons that day. She was quite sure he wouldn't be able to concentrate.

They had been fishing all morning. Now it seemed appropriate that they just let the bait sit, as it were, and see what might come of it.

As if pulled by Ruby and Fina's invisible magnetism, passengers began to emerge on deck. The pair had decided beforehand that the best course was to ignore everyone who came on deck – unless they initiated conversation.

Fina felt a little hand touch her arm. The first person to take them up on this offer was Victor, of course.

She pushed her sunglasses down and squinted at the little figure by her side. "Yes, Victor?" He held up a miniature pink pig. The pig had a devious, crooked smile and a gleam in his eye, but she decided Victor wouldn't notice or wouldn't care.

"Darling pig, Victor," she said. "Does your pig have a name?"

"Her name is Wendell," said Victor, looking affectionately at the pig.

Fina sat bolt upright, nearly knocking over her iced tea. Ruby looked over in surprise. Doing her best to calm down so as not to startle Victor into silence, Fina relaxed her shoulders and gently put her hand on Victor's shoulder.

"What a darling name for a pig, Victor. It is rather unusual for a pet name, however. How did you come up with it?"

Ruby was upright now, sitting on the edge of her lounge chair, straining to listen.

"I heard someone talking about Wendell yesterday and I liked the name."

Ruby said, "Who was talking about Wendell?"

Victor's face contorted in the effort of remembrance. Fina could tell he was enjoying the attention and was going to milk this scene for all that it was worth.

"Well, I heard someone mentioning it in the dining room yesterday – while we were making that smashing pea catapult," he said. Fina approved of his use of the word "smashing".

"You can't remember who it was?" asked Fina.

Violet Gibbs came rushing up to Victor, interrupting his concentration. Today she was wearing a pale green poplin afternoon dress. Fina was surprised that Violet could move that quickly, given her sickly condition.

"There you are, Victor," she said in a half-relieved, half-irritated voice. "We've been searching for you all over the ship. We were beginning to get worried. But now that we've found you, why don't you come join us with your pig. Gilbert has a pet cow so perhaps they can play together."

Removing her sunglasses so she could look directly at Violet, Ruby said, "Victor's pig is quite charming. Her name is Wendell." Ruby gave Violet a smile.

Fina's eyes locked on Violet's pasty face. Was it just her imagination, or did she see a flicker of her eyelids?

"Yes, charming, quite charming," she murmured as she led Victor away.

Ruby leaned back on her arms in mock disbelief. "Did I just hear that correctly?"

"Yes, you did, dear Ruby," responded Fina. She sipped her iced tea which was rapidly becoming hot tea. It was still refreshing.

Sipping her own iced tea through a straw, Ruby said, "Wendell the pig. So he heard someone talking about Wendell, which means that person was talking to someone else about Wendell. Does that mean there are two contacts on the ship?" She let out a sigh of frustration.

"It would seem that way. Should we be looking for pairs?"

"Well, there's the Gibbses, Emeline and Patricia, Ian and the captain, Lev and Neville, Ian and Balraj—"

"—and Balraj and Dolores. I suppose there might be some other configuration between Lev, Agnes, Sarah, and Neville."

"That's a lot of pairs, Feens. I don't know if that means we can eliminate any pairs connected to Balraj or not. I suppose we can eliminate – temporarily at least – Gibbs and Dolores because they weren't at dinner as pairs last night."

Fina held her head, as if it hurt. "I agree, but I'm so overwhelmed by even that list of suspects!"

Ruby nodded. "I agree. I think we need to make a list, but we need to do it out of sight. Let's go back to our cabin so we can talk about this before dinner. Especially because dinner will provide opportunities to ask more questions."

Fina scooped up her clutch and wriggled her feet into her sandals.

"Wait," hissed Ruby in a barely audible voice.

Fina scanned the horizon of the deck. She could see the Gibbses and Victor in one corner – all huddled underneath an umbrella as if they were in some sort of downpour. Except for Gilbert. He seemed to be setting some sort of insect on fire with a looking glass. Fina shuddered. Hopefully he was just looking at something closely.

Beyond that, she could see the outline of the bar toward the ship's stern. Lev was wiping down the bar and tables.

"What is it?" whispered Fina in disbelief. "It all looks calm to me."

Ruby gently motioned her head in the direction of the bar.

Neville rushed over to the bar, a large folder under his arm. He didn't acknowledge Lev's presence. That was decidedly odd, thought Fina, as Lev was a few tables away from the bar. But he didn't look up either, though he surely must have heard Neville's approach. If anything, he began to rub the table even more vigorously than before.

Neville left the folder on the top of the bar and loped down the deck.

Lev looked up from his spotless table, wiped his brow and made his way to the bar. He scooped up the envelope and slid it under his shirt. After gulping down a pink beverage on the bar, he shuffled off toward the stairs.

23

———

The chewy, gummy sweetness melted in Fina's mouth. "Thank you, Ruby. Exquisite," she said as she clenched her teeth on the next piece of dried mango.

"It is delectable, isn't it?" said Ruby, removing another piece from the handkerchief on the nightstand. "Ian gave me this bundle of mango this morning. We talked about it when we were at Pauncefort – I remember telling him how much I missed it."

"He is thoughtful, isn't he, Ruby?" Despite her jealousy of Ian and his somewhat suspicious behaviour, she liked him.

Ruby rubbed her nose. Fina knew what that meant. "He's just trying to cover for his odd behaviour – such as following us."

Washing down the mango with a large glass of water, Fina decided silence was enough of a response for now. She pulled out a full sheet of paper from the writing desk, rooted around for the pen, and then sat down to write.

"Thanks, Feens," said Ruby, wiping her sticky hands on a nearby handkerchief. "Let's try to organise our thoughts and then we can go back and take it all apart. Now, first – when might Balraj Chadha have been killed?"

Fina nodded, and wrote at the top of her sheet of paper: *What happened?*

Ruby said, "We know that he went to his cabin at 6:15. At 6:45, Agnes knocked and there was no answer."

"So he must've been killed between roughly 6:20 and 6:40," said Fina. She scrunched up her face. "That's not much time."

"I agree," said Ruby leaning back on the bed. "But let's assume it's possible at this point and move on from there. That means the people who could have done it would be Violet, Patricia, Emeline, Dolores, and possibly one of the staff. I suppose it could have been Lev or the captain, but it would have meant placing their careers in jeopardy."

Fina put down her pen. "So the murderer goes to Balraj's cabin, knocks, enters, carrying the weapon with them, and kills him. We still don't know what happened to the weapon."

Ruby tapped her teeth. "They must have hidden it, or carried it with them out of the cabin and thrown it overboard. I suppose either is possible. And how would the murderer know that Balraj would feel ill and go back to his cabin in the first place?"

"Exactly. We could suppose it's possible with extreme planning but that couldn't include predicting that Balraj would come back to his cabin early. On the other hand, if it were spur of the moment – because the murderer saw their opportunity – then they couldn't possibly have carried out the murder because it would take too much advance planning."

"We are definitely missing something that will allow us to go forward," said Ruby, staring at the ceiling. She sighed. "Let's look at the possible suspects."

Fina began to write.

Patricia Burbage: Did go downstairs during murder, to remove plantain from her hair. Unknown reason for killing him, though it was odd she asked for a séance. Something to do with her money?

Ian Clavering: Why is he on this trip? Acquaintance of Balraj. Odd behaviour. No real opportunity to commit murder during dinner.

Emeline Caulk: Did not go downstairs during dinner. No apparent motive for this murder, other than her generally frightful behaviour.

Dolores Dominguez: Has some sort of relationship with Balraj. Perhaps it went pear-shaped and she killed him? She did have opportunity because she sat out the dinner.

Phillip Gibbs: Did not go downstairs during murder, though perhaps he coordinated something with Violet? No apparent reason to kill Balraj, but perhaps he knew something about how they came by their treasure. Also – Balraj mentioned something in passing about the couple being "odd".

Violet Gibbs: Looks ill and thoroughly unhappy. Not enough to kill, though. Was downstairs during murder. Not sure she's well enough to hit Balraj on the head.

Gustave Marchand: Did not go downstairs during dinner. Was already friends – or at least acquaintances – with Balraj before the trip. Does his affable behaviour hide something?

Sadie Stiles: Did go downstairs with Victor during dinner, though she'd have to leave him to commit the murder. Seems implausible. Clearly upset with Balraj about something – enough to kill him? And what about that peculiar piece of paper about potatoes and grain?

Wrist aching, Fina put down her pen and wiped her brow. "What a conundrum," she sighed. "It seems impossible. And we have only two days – not even that – left to solve the murder."

"If we assume the murderer had to have been downstairs during dinner, then that narrows the suspects down to Patricia, Dolores, Violet and Sadie."

Fina shook her head. "I agree, but we just said that even if they somehow had enough time to commit the murder downstairs, how could they have known Balraj would return to his cabin?"

"Well, assuming the murderer just took the opportunity to actually follow Balraj without knowing he would leave beforehand, then that leaves us with precisely zero suspects. That's because Patricia didn't know she was going to be the recipient of Victor and Gilbert's plantain play, and Sadie didn't know she would need to take Victor downstairs," said Ruby with a small groan after she finished thinking aloud her conclusions.

A knock at the door saved Fina from having to agree with this dismal assessment of the investigation. "Come in!"

As she hastily turned the paper face down, the imposing figure of Patricia Burbage entered the room. Although the cabin was roomy, the woman somehow seemed to take up all the available space.

"Miss Burbage," said Ruby, putting on her best insincere smile. "How may we help you?"

This time, Patricia was in too much of a rush even to sniff. "I must apologise for disturbing you, but time is of the essence. You saw what happened at the séance," she said, spitting out the words rapid-fire. "The Ouija board confirmed what I already suspected. My life is in danger!"

Not again. Fina kept her mouth tightly shut. Let Ruby, with her diplomatic expertise, handle this one.

"I did see the séance," said Ruby, treading carefully, "but to my mind, there was no indication that you, Miss Burbage, are to be the next target."

"Did you not see what it spelt out? M-o-n-e-y! That was a clear reference to poor dear Henry and his fortune, which passed to me. Miss Dove," she cleared her throat, "I feel you are not taking this seriously. A Ouija board never lies, you know. And I have had other signs, other foreshadowings, which I have no doubt represent warnings from the Other Side."

Fina blinked.

"The Other Side," repeated Ruby. Even her legendary patience was wearing rather thin. Fina braced herself to step in.

"Correct," said Patricia grimly. "The captain has chosen not to take notice, but you mark my words." She leaned in closer. "There is an evil-doer on this ship, and that evil is coming for me!"

Without waiting for a reply, she turned and left, flinging the door shut with a decisive bang.

Leaning back in her chair, Fina let out a breath of relief. "That was spiffing, Ruby. I don't think I could have done it without calling her a liar."

Ruby allowed a small smile to creep across her face. "She certainly does seem to suffer from paranoia. But she's right about one thing."

"What's that? Not the bit about the Ouija board that never lies?"

"No. The bit about there being someone aboard this ship who is bent on doing evil."

24

The playing cards slid across the table, along with Fina's gin and tonic. The cards escaped, cascading to the floor in a gentle descent. The gin and tonic was held back, however, by those clever rails installed on the round tables in the green room.

She sipped the crisp G & T, savouring the sweet bitterness of the drink. Despite everything that had happened, she was enjoying herself. After a good supper and a liberal amount of wine, she felt everything was right in the world. Well, almost. Ruby looked as if she were enjoying herself too, imbibing a glass of white port.

Duke Ellington's 'Solitude' drifted from the gramophone in the corner.

Sadie lounged in a glorious pink and black muslin evening dress with a crossover cape. She twirled her pearl necklace between her fingers. Though she gave the physical appearance of attentiveness to Gustave's conversation, Fina could see by her slightly glazed eyes that her mind was elsewhere.

Phillip, Violet, Dolores and Ian played a lively game of bridge. Violet looked smashing in her white leather shoes, a black and white spotted dress, and a bow belt. Fina noticed a slight colour in Violet's cheeks for the first time. When it wasn't her turn, Violet rearranged the sugar bowl and shakers on the table, first in a line and then as a triangle.

Dolores held her jade cigarette holder steadily to her mouth. Though she appeared detached from the game, she still somehow managed to play. If Ian's grunts of approval were any indication, she was a good bridge partner.

Patricia and Emeline sat ensconced in a corner, backs to the wall. Emeline's carpet bag perched on her knees as if it were a cat. She perused some pamphlet or another. Fina could tell, even from this distance, that it was some sort of instructional manual – probably about how to protect the moral fitness of your pet.

Patricia seemed to be the only one who wasn't enjoying herself. Her amber brooch, in the shape of a spider, looked as if it might attack Emeline if it had the chance to jump off her lapel. Frowning, she sucked furiously on a cigarette in a scarlet holder. It seemed as if she couldn't get enough of the juice of the cigarette – Fina half expected her to remove it from the holder and begin chomping on it like a cigar. Instead, she persevered and quickly inserted another cigarette – as if her life depended on it.

Fina focused on Patricia, wondering if her wandering eye might find Sadie. As if on cue, Patricia's eyes scanned the room and began to stare at Sadie's neck. Clearly sensing the stare, Sadie's head swivelled around to stare back at Patricia – for just a moment before she returned to her conversation with Gustave.

Fina bent over to retrieve the recalcitrant cards. The ace of spades and the jack of diamonds. Ominous indeed.

Neville materialised to assist her. She was grateful for the help, as bending over in her alcohol-infused condition was not a brilliant idea. She held her head as she sat upright.

"Are you OK, Feens?" asked Ruby, taking a small sip of port. "A little too much G in your T?" she smiled.

"Yes, perhaps, but I feel quite wonderful!" replied Fina.

Neville gave a short smile. "Perhaps I should ask Lev to serve you some water, or some coffee?" he enquired.

"Certainly not," Fina retorted, feeling her neck grow warm. "I'm perfectly fine. Just a little tipsy. That's all."

Neville nodded and moved back to the bar. Lev rearranged glasses while Neville chatted with Agnes. Maxwell Mills seemed to be a very egalitarian captain, thought Fina. Then she thought perhaps this was due to the warm glow of the gin.

Lev loaded his tray with passengers' beverages of choice. Even though they had set sail only a few days ago, Fina already knew passenger preferences for beverages. Ruby had suggested that Fina should practise memorising details about situations and people. It would come in handy for their missions. Fina thought beverages would be a good way to start, especially because they sometimes revealed a hidden personality trait.

Gustave preferred a daiquiri. Sadie, ever the experimenter, had tried a sidecar earlier, but then requested a gimlet for this round. Emeline guzzled ginger beer like there was no tomorrow. Patricia preferred port – tawny port – but switched to white port when she saw it was available. Violet ordered a small neat rum, the cheapest drink available. Phillip ordered a Tom Collins, and Dolores requested a bourbon on the rocks. Fina thought that last drink said something about Dolores' personality, but she wasn't sure what it could be.

On impulse, Fina rushed to the bar. "Lev, could you make me a special drink? Your own creation?" He peered over the bar at her. Though he didn't smile, his mouth curved upward just enough to create a hint of a smile. "Certainly," he said. "You like cherries?"

"Oh yes. I adore cherries," she replied. "What is the drink called?"

He ignored her while he mixed his concoction. He placed the auburn liquid in a highball glass on the counter. Fina sipped it. "Mmm," she said in approval. "What's in it and what is it called?"

"Cognac, bitters and cherry liqueur. And it is called a Tarpan."

"It's delicious. What does 'tarpan' mean?"

"Ah, well, where I come from, it is a kind of horse."

Crash.

Metal clashing against metal made a tremendous racket from somewhere outside. This was followed by a screech and then a low growl.

Everyone rushed to the door. They all moved onto deck to see pots and pans rolling out of the kitchen. Sarah bent over and began to gather them up. Nearby, the same cat Ruby and Fina had seen earlier sat near the mountain of metal. The cat licked one paw slowly, back turned to Sarah.

"That damn cat! How did Souse get into my kitchen, I'd like to know?" she grumbled. Lev sprinted over to Sarah, but not before he gave Souse a friendly pat. Sarah did not look amused at his encouragement of such scandalous behaviour.

Drama at an end, the crowd moved back, en masse, into the green room. A great murmur of excited voices crescendoed and then died down as they all retook their places. Nerves were clearly on edge.

Neville distributed drinks around the room. His first stop was Ruby and Fina's table. He set down Fina's Tarpan with a half wink.

He moved around the room, deftly dodging moving chairs, limbs and the occasional casual hand flown out in a grand gesture with a cigarette attached. Delivering the last of the drinks to Emeline and Patricia's table, he returned to the bar.

Violet, who clearly had had one too many tots of rum, raised her glass in a toast. She rose from her seat, a little wobbly on her feet. Probably a combination of the drink and the swaying of the boat. Phillip touched her lightly on the hand and began to jiggle his leg at the same time – Fina couldn't tell if he was pulling her back down into her seat or giving her gentle encouragement. She decided it must be the former, given his rather alarmed expression.

"Dear friends, we have suffered tragedy but we shall pull through this together," she said, nearly hitting her husband in the head with her glass. Instinctively, Ruby and Fina glanced at each other. "Thank you to, a..." Fina winced in embarrassment for Violet as she grasped for Lev's name. "Ah, thank you to Lev for these wonderful drinks," she said, sloshing her drink in his direction at the bar. Lev couldn't help himself and broke out in a wide grin. Fina thought it clearly suppressed a laugh.

Without warning, a retching, writhing sound came from the corner of the room. A loud thud followed.

Fina swivelled round to see that one of the guests had collapsed upon the table, her head buried in the tablecloth, her arms hanging limp. It was Patricia. Her sister's mouth gawped in a soundless scream.

25

"Cyanide," pronounced Violet. She lowered the port glass onto the table as if it were a golden chalice.

Captain Mills strode into the room. He removed his cap as he came to a halt in front of Patricia's body, still slumped in that wholly unnatural position. Like a rag doll taking a nap on the table, thought Fina. Fortunately, Violet had gently closed Patricia's eyes. That stare was more than she could bear. Emeline, too, had fled into a corner of the room, where she sat with her back turned to the company, her head in her hands. The rest of the guests sat motionless, shocked into silence.

Except for Dolores. "Are you saying..." She could hardly bring herself to finish the thought. "There has been another murder?"

Ignoring her, Violet rose from the table. "I'm afraid Mrs Burbage has been poisoned, Captain Mills. Cyanide. In her port glass," she said.

"Thank you, Mrs Gibbs," replied the captain. "May I ask how you know it was cyanide? What I mean is, do you have special training in identifying poisons?"

With an odd little curtsy, she said, "I was a nurse during the war, sir. That's how I met Phillip," she said, nodding in her husband's direction. "I learned plenty about poisons in hospital. Cyanide is fairly easy to identify."

Emeline's harsh voice broke in. "You're a nurse? Is there anything you can do to, to, to save her?"

Violet shook her head in sympathy. "I'm sorry, Miss Caulk."

Ian stepped forward and put a hand on the captain's shoulder. He whispered into his ear.

At that, Emeline seemed to pull herself together. "Look here," she said, rising imperiously from her seat. "I do not appreciate this secret counsel about my sister's death. And who, who is this man to be whispering in your ear," she said, pointing a finger at Ian as if he were an apparition.

Her voice rose. "I demand an explanation!" Now her hand began to shake.

Violet, apparently transported back to her days of nursing the shell-shocked, rushed to Emeline's side and grasped her about the shoulders. This seemed to have the opposite of the intended calming effect. Emeline writhed and wriggled out of Violet's grasp. Once free, she leapt at the captain. She began to yell mild obscenities about "degenerates" and "delinquents". Ian looked toward Ruby and Ruby looked toward Lev. Ruby nodded. Then she looked to Fina. Fina gulped. Her insides began to churn like the butter she and her aunt used to make in her childhood.

Fina stepped up to Emeline's right, while Lev moved to her left. Emeline was oblivious to these machinations. Her hair shook and her face turned a pinkish shade of carmine. Fina inhaled a great gulp of air and nodded at Lev. They each slipped one arm up and over each of Emeline's flailing arms and moved them to her side. In one deft, coordinated movement, Fina and Lev began to shift Emeline away from the captain.

At first, Emeline moved with them. Then she went limp,

nearly collapsing on top of Fina. The sudden pressure of her considerable weight nearly made Fina wobble and fall like a newborn foal. Thankfully, her muscles bore up under her. Feeling grateful for the fitness-boosting tennis lessons she had taken back in Oxford, she managed to help Lev drag Emeline to one of the bench-cum-sofas near the farthest exit.

By this time, Emeline had begun to babble. Unfortunately, there were a number of words mixed into her incoherencies that were rather too coherent. Dolores sidled up to the bar and swiped a glass full of liquid and strode toward Emeline, as if she were an angry giraffe. Then, leaning back with her glass, she swept it forward in one quick gesture, splashing water directly in Emeline's face. She turned and waltzed her way back to her seat.

Fina and Lev had loosened their grip on Emeline, mostly to avoid the small tsunami of water. The cold shock had worked. Emeline sat, stunned and quiet, with water dripping down her face.

No one apparently felt Dolores' action was beyond the bounds of propriety – if they did, they dared not say anything.

The captain unbuttoned his blazer and wiped his brow. "As I was about to say, I know this second tragedy aboard has us all rattled—"

"To say the least!" interjected Phillip, chewing furiously on his pipe. "Sir, this is outrageous!"

"Yes, quite so," replied the captain. "We are now approximately two days away from arriving at our destination. In the meantime, I've asked Mr Clavering," he said, pointing to Ian, as if not everyone might be aware of who he was, "and Miss Dove and Miss Aubrey-Havelock to investigate what appear to be two murders." He held up his hand to pre-empt any protests from the passengers.

"They all, ah, have experience in these *matters*," he said with emphasis on the last word. Scanning the room, Fina stopped at the Gibbses' faces. They didn't have a look of guilt, but rather one of injury – perhaps because they hadn't been asked to be a part of the investigation team? Dolores' face still looked indignant, a sure holdover from her encounter with Emeline. Sadie's mouth twisted, as if she couldn't comprehend the situation. Fina felt the same way.

Gustave's face held no trace of expression, as usual, but she did see that his left hand shook as he adjusted his tie. The staff were all present now as well, except Neville. Fina guessed he was on deck in case of an emergency.

Agnes sat in a chair at the bar, head in hand, gazing at the captain with glassy eyes. Sarah stood next to her, rhythmically sliding her bracelets up and down her arm. The rather loud sighing sounds coming from her direction indicated impatience. Though she couldn't see Lev's face as Emeline's now frozen and quiet body blocked her view, she could sense he was at ease.

A strong breeze rushed through the room, overturning one of the glasses nearest the captain. It splintered into a hundred shards on the floor. Everyone jumped. Even Emeline awoke from her stupor and began to mumble gibberish under her breath. Agnes began to move toward the sparkling mess on the floor out of instinct.

The captain held up his hand again. "Please, no one must touch anything in this room except those I have mentioned. I know the crew will assist you in any way possible," he said, nodding toward the staff. "And I expect full cooperation from all of the passengers. While we are at sea, I act in the role of a legal authority. Please understand that and we shall all stay safe. I suggest you all return to your cabins and lock your doors." He made as if to leave, then spoke over his shoulder.

"And please be careful when answering the door."

26

"Mrs Gibbs – would you stay behind?" asked Ruby as passengers began to file out of the room.

Ian gave a quick glance at Ruby. Fina couldn't tell if it was one of surprise or irritation at Ruby's request.

Violet's face looked as if it belonged to a fully living, breathing person now. She must be pleased by the excitement, the feeling of worth coming from her nursing skills or was it from something else?

"I'd be glad to be of assistance – if that's possible, of course," replied Violet.

The small group of investigators, comprised of the captain, Ian, Ruby, Violet and herself, moved toward the limp body. Fina noticed that Patricia's hair was as perfect as ever. Indeed, everything about her was perfect, even in death. The one exception was her brooch: the amber spider that now looked grotesque on the body, creeping toward Patricia's face. Fina shuddered.

The captain scratched his head. "If we don't need the body here, I'll ask Lev and Agnes to move Mrs Burbage to... ah... cold storage. I think it's best that we do that as quickly as possible. It's supposed to get quite warm tomorrow," he finished with a grimace.

The captain left the green room in search of Lev and Agnes, who had left along with the passengers. Ruby began to collect all the drinks glasses on Lev's silver tray.

"I suppose anyone could have dropped the cyanide into her glass," said Ian, taking a seat in the nearest chair.

"Mm-hm," said Fina. "The murderer could have slipped it in during the commotion. We all left the green room to see what was happening in the kitchen." She could see from the tilt of Ruby's head that she was listening to their dialogue, even as she focused on gathering the motley assortment of glasses.

With the deft, pincher-like motion of a crab, Ian withdrew a handkerchief from his breast pocket. He began to mop up the sweat on his brow, then moved the handkerchief over the top of his close-cropped hair. Fina could tell it was an act of consternation rather than a mere hygienic chore.

Finishing her task, Ruby placed the tray in front of Violet. Then she sat down next to Violet and said, "Let's each sniff each glass." Violet looked at her quizzically.

"I study chemistry at Oxford," said Ruby, clearly enjoying the look of astonishment on Violet's face. Fina also noticed Ian's amusement at the comment.

Methodically, they stuck their noses in each glass. Meanwhile, Ian retrieved the bottle of white port. He set it down at the end of the neat line of drinks to be tested. Most of the glasses still contained their original liquids. Fina watched as Violet and Ruby sniffed and then shook their heads at each glass in turn. Violet placed one glass after another in an orderly row. They had already determined that the cyanide was in Patricia's glass – the lack of poison in the other glasses indicated she was indeed the intended victim.

Squeak. Ian pulled the cork out of the port bottle. He

handed the bottle to Ruby and said, "You'd better check this." Ruby's eyes widened and the corners of her mouth drew downwards. She stayed silent while she handed the bottle to Violet. After sniffing the neck of the bottle, Violet's expression mirrored that of Ruby's.

"It's cyanide," said Violet, knowing no other explanation was needed.

Ruby shifted in her seat. She smoothed her dress and her hair. "But I was drinking from this bottle, too."

Fina's stomach lurched as her photographic memory shifted back to their first round of drinks. "You were the one who first ordered port, remember?"

Ruby nodded. "Yes, that's right. Patricia had put in an order for a sidecar and changed her mind after she saw me enjoying the white port. She had never had white port and wanted to try it."

"But did everyone hear her say that?" asked Ian.

"I believe so," said Violet, who then looked embarrassed, or perhaps guilty, that she remembered, thought Fina.

"Lev took the bottle from behind the bar," said Ruby slowly, "and poured me a glass. He left it on the bar until a bit later, when Patricia asked for one. We were all milling around and chatting. Anyone could have had access to the bottle."

"And later, might you have asked for a second glass from that same bottle?" asked Fina, already knowing the answer.

"Why, yes," answered Ruby. "Yes, I might."

"Well, that just about tears it," said Ian. "I'd lay good money that you were the intended target. This means I'll be standing on watch in front of your door all night, Ruby."

27

Click.

The sound of the bolt sliding into the lock on their door felt reassuring. Fina slid a small but heavy footrest in front of the door, more for peace of mind rather than as any real bulwark against an intruder.

Ruby had rejected Ian's offer of night-time protection – mostly out of pride, thought Fina. Perhaps it was her lingering resentment of Ian's peculiar behaviour on this trip. He certainly seemed to be acting more "normally" – whatever that might be – since their little coterie of investigators had formed.

Ruby and Fina sat on their knees in their cabin, working away on their latest project. Colourful dots made by Ruby's straight pins – the type used for fittings – decorated the far wall. The pins held scraps of paper filled with scribblings and question marks. They had removed the paintings from that wall to make it their official investigation palette.

Ruby gave out a sigh of what seemed to be satisfaction as they stuck the last bits of paper on the wall. Fina admired the rather artistic effect of a pointillist painting – perhaps Seurat?

Except it didn't seem to add up to much of anything in terms of content or shape.

To the left was their original list of suspects in Balraj's murder. As she looked at it now, Fina reflected that it seemed less conclusive than ever. Certainly it was failing to suggest to her the definitive clue to the killer's identity.

To the right was their latest effort: a similar list, except this time for the second murder. It was based on the assumption that the murderer was after Patricia, not Ruby. This list was less helpful because everyone could have poisoned Patricia, thought Fina.

Ian Clavering: No apparent reason to poison her. She did have millions, though, so maybe there's some connection to his strange behaviour?

Emeline Caulk: Definite reason to kill her sister for money and her pet causes.

Dolores Dominguez: No apparent reason.

Phillip Gibbs: No apparent reason. The Gibbses must have money, so it cannot be connected to Patricia's warnings about money! Perhaps they were worried by the séance where the word "money" came up — that Patricia knew about their treasure?

Violet Gibbs: Same as Phillip. Did seem to be healthier right before Patricia was poisoned. A connection there?

Gustave Marchand: No apparent reason.

Sadie Stiles: No apparent reason. They travel in similar circles, so maybe there's some unknown connection? Sexual tension between her and Patricia.

"Hmph," said Fina.

"Hmph what?"

"Sadie seems like such a marvellous person. Raising her son on her own and all that. And she is rather kind."

"Every grin is not laughter, Feens."

"You have a point. I am biased."

Fina shifted to gaze at the wall again. "What about the staff? Some of them have been acting oddly."

"I agree," said Ruby, yawning. "But we don't have any motives for them. And their peculiarity might be tied to our mission more than to the murders." Seeing the look of scepticism on Fina's face, Ruby continued, "I'm not saying I don't think they could have done it – just that they lack motives."

She frowned and began to pace across a well-worn path in the rug. Apparently previous passengers were habitual pacers as well. Fina knew what this meant. Ruby was puzzled, deeply puzzled by some aspect of the case that didn't "fit".

"Let's go, Feens," she said as she tucked her feet into her slippers near the bed. "Could you take that torch Ian gave us before bed?"

Fina responded by putting on her own slippers and locating the torch in her bag. "Where are we going?"

"To Balraj's room again. I know it's devilishly creepy."

"You cannot be serious."

"The answer to his murder – and perhaps to Patricia's – lies in that room. I'm sure of it," Ruby said, holding up the key to Balraj's room in triumph. Pre-empting Fina's question, she said, "Ian gave me one of the spare keys."

They approached Balraj's cabin. As soon as Ruby tapped the door lightly with her gloved fingers, it creaked open. Had the captain left it open on purpose?

Outside Balraj's room on the deck, Fina could hear the gentle lapping of the waves. The deck was lit by a half-moon, the milky light filtering through passing clouds overhead. While Ruby fiddled with the torch, Fina closed her eyes and felt the swaying of the boat. Taking a deep breath and opening her eyes, she convinced herself that she could get past her fears of going into a murdered man's cabin in the dead of night. But not the fears that the murderer was after Ruby.

Bang.

Fina jumped, grabbing Ruby's arm. This caused them to tumble, head over heels, into Balraj's room. Ruby leapt up and shut the door so rapidly that it made a whooshing noise. The door clicked shut. Smoothing her hair, she bent down to whisper to Fina. "It was just the wind banging shut a door. I'm sure of it."

Fina blinked.

Then she gave Ruby what she hoped was a reassuring smile. She certainly wasn't reassured. But she knew she had to push on, so she scooped up the torch that had escaped Ruby's grasp and rose from her cramped position on the floor. Leaning over, she pulled the curtains – rather reluctantly as the moon seemed to be the one pleasant aspect of their escapade this evening – so that the light from the torch couldn't be seen easily from outside.

Realising she had no idea what they were searching for, she handed the torch to Ruby. Ruby shone it around the room. First, on the desk with the sundry colourful bottles, watch, stationery, pens and parrot. Second, she shone the torch clockwise onto the door and the little ledge above with the wooden turtle. Third, past the window to the nightstand with the carafe of water and a water glass. Fourth, in a lightning motion back to the floor where the body had lain. The rug looked the same as it had been before.

Ruby crouched down by the rug as if she were about to leap like a frog. She shook her head. From her pursed lips, Fina could see she was bewildered rather than disappointed. Fina supposed this was a somewhat positive sign.

"Feens," she hissed. "This isn't what I expected. It's very frustrating!"

"What's frustrating?"

But before Ruby had a chance to reply, a scratching, tapping noise came from the door, as if a small dog were trying to enter the room.

They froze.

28

Ruby and Fina crouched behind the door. The handle slowly turned. A beam of light from a torch shined in through a crack in the moulding.

The torchlight danced round the room as a figure slipped in. It tiptoed toward the bathroom.

Ruby flicked on the light switch. "Ian!" she exclaimed, clutching her chest. "What a fright you gave us!" She rushed at him with such intensity that Fina thought she might hit him.

He turned, his face rather ashen. He clutched his own chest. "You're not the only one who's had a fright," he said.

Fina knew she had a sceptical expression on her face. Ian glanced at her and said, "I heard noises coming from this cabin – I was walking about the boat, hoping for a glimpse of the murderer. Besides," he said, switching off his torch, "I couldn't sleep."

"There are a couple of things that are puzzling me about this room, Ian," said Ruby. "That's why Fina and I came to search again."

"Do you mean the puzzle of why the murderer bothered to clean up after themselves when it was quite obvious that Balraj was murdered?" he asked as Ruby began to pull back the covers on the perfectly undisturbed bed.

"Exactly. It doesn't make any sense, especially because time was of the essence in this crime. How in the world would the murderer be able to clean up anything in the space of what – twenty minutes total?" She looked carefully at the bed linens, finding nothing. "I wanted to eliminate the possibility that he was killed while in bed," she explained, with a final gesture of pulling up the bedclothes.

"Are you sure Balraj was killed in those twenty minutes?" asked Ian, returning to the previous question.

"I don't see when else it could have occurred," said Fina. "Especially because there was no answer when Agnes left the tray. Why else would Balraj request dinner be served and then not take the meal? He couldn't have fallen asleep that quickly."

"I suppose he could have been drugged at dinner and then fallen asleep," said Ian.

"That seems too risky," replied Ruby. "Though I agree that our murderer does enjoy taking enormous risks."

Fina's eyes grew wide with a new realisation. "You don't think he was poisoned and then hit on the head to make it look like that was the way he was killed, do you?"

Ian's eyebrows began to wiggle. "You're on to something there, Fina. That's got to be the answer. What do you think, Ruby?" he said, gazing at her with anticipation.

Ruby bit her lip and lowered herself into the nearest chair. All that pacing must have exhausted her.

"It's certainly an ingenious idea, and I would probably have used it myself if I were the murderer," she said with a wan smile. "But there's no sign of poisoning. If he had been given cyanide, for example, it would take very little time for it to take effect."

Fina frowned. "Yes, and even if there were some slow-acting poison, the problem is that we weren't served water or cocktails at our table until after Balraj had left. I remember that quite distinctly. Others at our table did have cocktails but those were drinks they had brought with them from the bar."

Ian stood near the nightstand, surveying the carafe of drinking water which was now lined with little stagnation bubbles. He smelled the carafe and the water glass next to it. He handed them to Ruby. She sniffed them as if they had a delicate bouquet and shook her head. Then she popped into the bathroom – presumably to look for glasses there – but came back quickly without any news to report.

As if she were a builder, Ruby began to triangulate different points in the room, looking from one point to another. Then with a rapid movement, she strode up to Ian. She stood level with him. Close. Eye-to-eye.

"If we're going to continue, I need to trust you."

Ian backed away. Ruby was so near to him that his only option was to bend backward and then move, nearly causing him to stumble. Fina had never seen him so flustered before. "W-what do you mean?"

"Wendell."

Ian's eyes moved side to side. "Wendell?"

"You heard me the first time, Ian," said Ruby in a low voice. Fina knew that voice. It meant someone was treading on dangerous ground.

Shoulders gradually lowering like the Caribbean temperature at night, Ian replied in a firm and confident voice. "Miss Ruby Dove, I have no idea what you're talking about."

Her eyes narrowed. "Mr Ian Clavering, is that the truth?"

"Yes." He spread his arms helplessly. "Yes! What do I have to do to convince you?"

But Ruby was already convinced – Fina could see it in the set of her chin. Ian had not been let into the secret of their code word. That wasn't enough for Ruby to let him off the hook, however.

"I still feel we're owed an explanation."

Ian plopped down on the bed next to Fina. "You were right to be suspicious of my reasons for being here."

"I knew it," said Ruby.

"I had a friend tell me you two were going on this trip. After our encounter at Pauncefort Hall, I suspected you might be on, shall we say – a mission?"

Ruby was silent. Fina blinked.

"A 'friend'?" asked Fina, seeing by Ruby's clenched jaw that she was experiencing a wave of emotions she was trying hard to hold back. "What do you mean, 'friend'?"

"A friend in the service. His Majesty's service," he said flatly.

Ruby shot up like a pop-goes-the-weasel. She began to pace again. "I knew it! I knew you must be an agent. How could I have been so trusting?"

"Well, if it's any consolation, you weren't exactly trusting," said Ian with a grin.

"How dare you!" she said, voice rising and then lowering. "You played on my feelings to get information."

Fina thought she should slip into the bathroom. She felt like a fifth wheel.

Ian gestured as if to stop Ruby. "I can explain. When I said I had a friend in the service, I meant just that. It does not mean I work for the service."

"Well, who do you work for?" asked Ruby.

Ian held up his hands in exasperation. "I wish I could tell you, I really do. But I can assure you it is not for the British Empire – in any form."

"Then why would you follow us?" asked Fina.

He turned to Fina. "I have my reasons. Truly."

She stared back at him.

He sighed. "All right. If I'm perfectly honest, my primary purpose here is not to keep tabs on you two. There are certain other people on this ship who are, shall we say, persons of inter-est. I've been asked to keep an eye on their activities."

Holding up a hand as if to pre-empt protests, he said, "And I cannot tell you any more than that. My plans don't interfere with your plans, whatever they might be," he said. "With or without, er, this Wendell character."

Ruby groaned, but her jaw began to relax, ever so slightly. "You are an exasperating man, Mr Ian Clavering."

29

Fina peeled open her eyes the next morning. She heard a slith-ering noise. Bolt upright now, she peered over the foot of her bed, by the door.

A rather crumpled but still neatly folded piece of paper lay on the floor. She let out a sigh of relief that the paper wasn't something more sinister and slid out of bed. Rubbing her eyes, she padded over to the door.

As Fina bent over and scooped up the paper, her head began to swim. She felt as if she had a thumping great hangover, but she hadn't had that much to drink yesterday. Then came a wave of nausea. She ran to the nightstand and began to gulp down water from the pitcher. Feeling better, she sat and then lay back in bed. Good, she thought, the room isn't spinning.

Taking in a deep breath of air, she opened the piece of paper. Her hands shook. Was it going to be a warning from the murderer? Fina admonished herself again for jumping to the worst-case scenario – as she was wont to do.

The note, scrawled in large black capitals, read: *Dear Miss Ruby I must speak to you. Agnes.* Next to her own name, Agnes had drawn a door in great detail. The door was open.

Fina sat bolt upright and whispered, "Ruby, Ruby, wake up." Silence. Fina's heart stopped.

Leaping out of bed, she tripped on the bedclothes and nearly ended up on her head. Now the adrenaline was really coursing through her body.

She grabbed Ruby's arm and began to shake her.

"Mmm. What is it?" Ruby said, turning over on her side, eyes still closed.

Fina let out a great sigh of relief.

"Agnes just left us a note. It's urgent."

Ruby's eyelids slid backwards almost into her head. She grasped at the sheet of paper as she lifted her head to read it. For several moments she clutched it, frowning. Then her head fell back with a sigh. It sounded like a sigh of irritation rather than fear or relief.

"Of course. Agnes! I knew this would happen. I wish I had thought to talk to her earlier. Let's get a move on."

Fina bit her lip. "You'd better go without me. I have been neglecting my duties as a governess – even though circumstances dictated that."

Ruby nodded. "You're right. You go ahead next door and I'll get dressed. Then I'll find Agnes. We mustn't waste a moment. If she knows what I think she knows, she could be in serious danger."

The look on Ruby's face was enough to warn Fina not to question her. Instead, she quickly slipped into a blue Chesro summer frock and got ready to make the short journey next door. As she opened the door, she exclaimed, "Look, Ruby. Ian brought us breakfast." She picked up the tray with the large note that read *From Ian* and breathed in the aromas of island sweetbread, plantains, toast, eggs and coffee.

Fina brought in the tray and slid it onto the desk. With a sweeping hand gesture, she said, "There you are. A proper breakfast. I could use one too. Mind if I swipe a bit of toast and marmalade before I go next door?" Fina said it as if Ruby could deny the request.

She plucked a piece of toast out of the rack and dipped a knife into the marmalade. As she began to spread it across the toast, Ruby picked up the breakfast card that read *From Ian* and held it close to her face.

"Wait!" she yelled, grabbing Fina's hand. "It's poisoned!"

The toast clattered onto the plate.

"Poisoned!" gasped Fina. "How do you know?" She noticed that her own hand was quivering.

"I didn't ask for any breakfast. Did you?"

"No, but—"

"Besides, anyone could have tampered with this tray since it was set out in the corridor."

Fina glared at the toast with distrust. "But no one could poison a rack of toast, could they? Would they? Ruby, you're beginning to sound like Patricia."

Ruby snorted. "Yes, and look what happened to her. Besides, the poison would be in the marmalade. And Fina..." She waved the card. "This isn't Ian's handwriting."

"Good gracious. I hadn't thought of that – obviously," said Fina. "Selkies and kelpies!" she added, recoiling from the tray. "You'd better come with me to look in on Victor – you shouldn't be on your own."

Fina saw Ruby hesitate, draw herself up in a defiant gesture, and then let out great gush of air. "You're right."

After tapping lightly on Sadie and Victor's door, Fina saw a little head appear between the curtains in the window. Victor saw Ruby and Fina and gave out a big grin. He opened the door a crack and peeked out.

"Mama's asleep," he whispered. "I'm playing with Wendell. She's in school with Robby and Torty, and they're having lessons." He gestured behind him to where the malevolent pig sat alongside a porcelain robin and his cabin's wooden turtle. They were all lined up in a neat row, each with a tiny scrap of paper and shard of pencil lead before it.

Fina nodded her approval. "I'm glad you checked to see who it was before you opened the door. Ruby and I wanted to make sure you didn't need anything. Did you have your breakfast?"

"Yes! We ate and Mama said she wanted to lie down."

"We'll see you later, Victor," said Ruby, tousling his hair. They waited until Victor had closed the door and turned the bolt, and then went in search of Agnes.

It was another perfectly blue, sunny day. The sea was flat. Too flat. Like walking through sticky, gooey treacle, thought Fina. The lack of air circulation, even on deck, meant it was hard to find relief anywhere on the ship. Most passengers – perhaps despite their better judgment – were scattered around the ship in small groups. Anywhere there might be a little friendly breeze.

"Keep your eyes open," Ruby whispered in Fina's ear. "If that marmalade was really poisoned, someone here is going to be very surprised to see us up and walking about."

"Good thought!" Fina whispered back. "Let's take a promenade around the deck a few times. We may find Agnes cleaning one of the cabins – and we can see who reacts to our presence."

But no one leapt out of their chairs, or even raised an eyebrow, as they strolled along. Dolores and Gustave were in the lounge, near the door. Emeline was in the reading room, staring blankly at a book through her pince-nez. Lev was mopping the deck with furious abandon, so much so that it made his hedgehog tattoo look like it was running and jumping. Only the Gibbses were absent.

Ruby and Fina strode toward the stairs that led to the crew's quarters. As they passed the Gibbses' cabin, Fina noticed the door was ajar, ever so slightly. She glanced up and down the deck and then motioned to Ruby to stand outside the door to listen.

"Soon we'll be safe. No need to worry," said Phillip in a whisper. Violet sounded like she had a cold or had been crying. "I hope so, Phillip, for all our sakes."

Out of the corner of her eye, Fina saw Neville moving toward them with a rapid step. She turned to Ruby and began talking to her as if they had just stopped in front of the Gibbses' door for a chat with each other. She could feel herself making exaggerated gestures and wondered if Neville was fooled. Did it really matter?

She felt Neville tap her on the shoulder. Spinning round, she held a fixed expression of surprise on her face as if this were the most unanticipated event in the world.

Neville wiped his brow. "Fina and Ruby, I'm glad I found you."

They both now stood at attention. Fina could tell from his ramrod-straight posture that something was wrong. Very wrong.

"Agnes has vanished."

30

Fina's mouth hung open as wide as that of the fish served at last night's dinner.

"Vanished?" she repeated, as if she had not heard the word. The familiar knot of dread tightened her stomach.

Neville nodded and kept nodding. He couldn't stop.

Ever self-possessed, Ruby put an arm around Neville's shoulder. "When did you notice she was missing?"

"This morning. She wasn't at breakfast. Agnes never misses breakfast. She's the first one there and the last one to leave."

"Has the captain been informed?" asked Fina.

"Yes, that was the first thing I did. He ordered an immediate search of all rooms. That's what I'm about to do. He said that we were not even to inform the guests, but get on with it immediately. Of course, you two are different..."

One side of Ruby's face rose, conveying scepticism. "Our cabins are so tiny that it would be impossible to hide ah, Agnes, and not think the bod—, I mean she, would be discovered soon." She paused. "But I understand the captain's impulse to do so. It should keep the murderer distracted for a while, if nothing else."

Fina and Neville nodded in unison at her statement.

She continued, "Neville, I assume you, Lev and Sarah will conduct this search?"

"Yes. Ian will also be joining us. Sarah, however, will be working in the kitchen. She says cooking soothes her nerves. She is in a foul temper. And how could I blame her? We're all on edge."

Fina held her head with both hands. This trip had been only four days, but it certainly felt like four years. Breathe, Fina, she told herself. Everything will be fine. Soon we'll be in Trinidad and this will all be sorted.

"Feens?" said Ruby, grasping Fina's shoulders.

She looked up at Ruby, who looked like she could use a hug herself. They took deep breaths in unison.

"We're going to get through this," said Fina, as much to herself as to Ruby.

"Yes," said Ruby, straightening up. She turned to Neville.

"Have you searched thoroughly in the crew's quarters downstairs yet?" she asked.

"More of a quick search," he replied. "I didn't look under beds and the like as I thought she must be cleaning one of the rooms upstairs."

"I think it's time to search under beds," said Ruby, teeth clenched.

After the trio had searched the crew's sleeping quarters, kitchen and engine room, they came to the utility room. It reeked of washing powder and mothballs. Dim light filtered from a buzzing lightbulb. Along the wall stood two wash basins. They pushed aside layers of linens hanging from clotheslines as if they were walking through dense underbrush.

And then Fina saw it. The heel of a shoe, a white shoe. The colour of the shoe camouflaged it among the white sheets.

Unconsciously, she began to double over in anticipation of what was connected to that shoe.

She said nothing but pointed at the heap of linens.

Neville reached the pile of linen first. He lifted the sheets gingerly to reveal a leg. As he began to reveal more, Fina turned away.

"It's Agnes, all right," breathed Neville. "It looks as if she's been hit on the head, but I think she's still alive."

Ruby rushed out of the room as soon as Neville had finished his sentence. As she ran, she yelled, "Going to fetch Violet!"

Neville and Fina dug through the pile of linen around Agnes as gently as they could, uncovering her motionless body. Fina felt an all-too-familiar raw acid creeping up her oesophagus. As if he could sense she was going to need to leave the room, Neville said, "Fina, please find the captain. He'll need to know what happened. I'll make Agnes comfortable until Mrs Gibbs arrives."

Grateful for this method of escape, Fina leapt up from her crouched position. Instantly she knew she had leapt up too quickly. The room began to swim. Then everything went black.

31

Something tickled her cheek. Then her arms. A cool dampness descended on her forehead.

Fina blinked as a hand moved the washcloth across her face.

Emeline stared down at her. "How are you feeling, Fina?" she said in a soft voice. Emeline smiled. Fina had never seen Emeline smile, so it was rather disconcerting – it was as if she were trying it for the first time. Her thin lips were pulled back so far they revealed her pale gums.

Now Fina's eyes were wide open. She was back in her own cabin. "What, what happened? I remember Agnes…"

"Shhh, there now, dear. Just rest. Here's some tea. It will make you feel much better," she said, tipping a steaming cup toward Fina's mouth.

Fina tried to rise, not to drink the tea, but to move out of this vulnerable position. Emeline's hands held her fast on the bed.

"Let go!" cried Fina, waving her hands which caused the teacup to tumble to the floor.

Emeline sat back, stunned. "I was just trying to help, dear."

Fina gave Emeline's facial expression and body language her full attention. What on earth was different about her? Her posture, while still straight, was not rigid. Her hands lay in her lap, naturally, rather than being balled into fists. And her face – well, it seemed softer, as if someone had ironed out those wrinkles that come with worry or personalities determined to set the world right.

"Where is Ruby and why are you here?" she demanded.

Emeline's mouth transformed into that wolf-like smile again. "Ruby and the others are attending to Miss Gidge. I offered my room since, since Patricia isn't there." Her eyes began to well up. This was the first time Fina thought Emeline had displayed genuine emotion rather than a reaction. "Years ago, I also acted as a nurse – even though I've had no formal training – for our mother and father during their long declines in health."

The knot in Fina's stomach began to loosen a bit. Her survival urge to leave the cabin dissipated. Something odd was going on, certainly, but she wasn't in immediate danger.

Emeline paused. She stared at the crack in the ceiling and then at the sea, visible through a small opening in the curtains. She looked like a woman contemplating a difficult decision.

"Thank you for tending to me while the rest of the ship is in an uproar. Is there something wrong, something I can help you with?" prompted Fina.

Emeline crooked her finger and beckoned Fina closer. It was all too reminiscent of Little Red Riding Hood, but she moved closer anyway. Bending toward her so her chair tipped at an angle, Emeline whispered one word, directly in her ear.

"Wendell."

Then Emeline sat back, rocking her tilted chair into place. A look of sly satisfaction passed over her face. No doubt it was in reaction to her own expression, thought Fina.

Fina clutched at the bedclothes, as if grabbing onto something would help her make sense of Emeline's simple statement. Though her mind raced, it failed to reach any conclusion, instead spinning round in circles. Was this some sort of trap? What would Ruby do? Why had Emeline told her, Fina, rather than telling Ruby? After all, Wendell was Ruby's brother. And what about Emeline's horrible projects?

Fina shook her head and closed her eyes. None of this made any sense.

Emeline, probably sensing her confusion, began to offer some answers. "You must be puzzled about why I'm telling you rather than Ruby."

Fina blinked, not wanting to give anything away, but still willing her to continue.

Emeline crossed her legs casually – certainly a gesture Fina had never seen her engage in before. Rummaging around in her carpet bag, she looked triumphant as she pulled out a packet of Woodbine cigarettes and a silver lighter.

"You smoke?!" asked Fina. She couldn't help herself. This transformation was too much.

Emeline smiled again. With each successive smile, it looked more natural – like the way other people smile. She must be easing back into character, thought Fina. But which one of these characters was real? The old or the new Emeline?

Leaning back while blowing smoke away from Fina's face, Emeline said, "Yes, dear Fina. I smoke. I drink. I have fun, believe it or not. I see by your face that my little transformation has you quite puzzled. As we're unlikely to be disturbed for a while, I will give you the full story."

"Please do," said Fina, confident that agreeing wouldn't give anything away.

"As for the first question – about why I said 'Wendell' to you rather than Ruby – that's because if anyone saw me talking to Ruby, it would 'blow my cover' as the Americans say. I had built up an image that protected me, as well as the two of you, so I had to keep it up," she said, tipping ash into an unused ashtray on the nightstand. Neither Fina nor Ruby smoked.

"You mean to say that your character – the original Emeline – was all an act?"

"Absolutely, my dear. You see, it isn't hard for me to pretend, because that used to be my genuine character. That's who I really was, up until about five or six years ago."

"What happened then to change you?"

"I was a missionary – the details will bore you. I had some realisations about British money interests and the ways people were treated. And I fell in love."

Fina suppressed a giggle. She felt guilty, but the thought of the original Emeline falling in love seemed completely at odds with her old personality. The only way she knew how to quash the burbling laughter inside of her was to ask another question. "And that forever changed you?"

"Didn't something change you, dear Fina? Those of us born with blinkers have to have something shake us into consciousness."

Fina nodded. Oh yes, she had had a number of experiences in her life that shook her. It was cumulative for her, however, rather than a single event.

Emeline smiled, guessing that Fina did not want to share any of these stories with the rather peculiar old or new Emeline.

"To make quite a long story short, I joined in *the cause*, as you might say. That's why I'm here today, telling you Wendell's name. I know in due course, after you've had time to tell Ruby, that you'll make sure I get whatever it is you're supposed to pass along to me."

"But wait, why are you telling me now? And how could you fool your sister?"

"Well, I don't think any of us expected a murder to occur, let alone two, plus the attempted murder of Miss Gidge. I know I've been acting suspiciously, so I figured I'd better tell you two – since you are investigating these crimes – before things spiralled out of control even more."

As she talked, Fina played back a photographic reel of Emeline's behaviour in her mind. "Yes, I can see that you were putting on an act, but why were you so flustered about your manuscript?"

Emeline's eyes dilated with excitement. "I'm a writer."

"Yes," said Fina. "Go on."

"I write pulp fiction. You two saw my manuscript."

"Why that's fabulous, Emeline!" said Fina, really meaning it.

"You think so?" Emeline sounded like a dog seeking approval. "I do rather enjoy it – and make a modest income from it. My pen name is Jack Juliano."

Fina cleared her throat. "How about my second question – about fooling your sister?"

Emeline's face contorted with grief. "She was a rather silly woman, but she was still my sister. I shall miss her a great deal," she sniffed, her eyes turning glassy. "It was quite easy to keep up the act with her – if that's what it's called – since that's the way she always thought of me. But this business with her oil shares limited my ability to act the part. The worker deaths and the like. I think she suspected something wasn't quite right, although I don't know that for sure."

"How did she act differently?"

"I wasn't as fulsome in my praise of her as I had been in the past – as I'm her big sister. It wasn't anything definite, but there was a growing distance between us. Ironically, I think she thought I wanted her money for my various causes."

"Well, she certainly seemed to be on the defensive. She gave us plenty of warnings."

Emeline's eyes bulged. "What do you mean? What warnings? About her death?"

"Yes, she said that she was in danger – that someone wanted to take her life. I'm not sure why, but I'm certain the threat must have been from an acquaintance. That is, someone who wasn't her sister."

"That's possible. It could account for her being on edge. Perhaps I misinterpreted her distance from me – maybe she had other things on her mind."

"It could have been both, but I think there was more to it – especially because whoever threatened her carried out their promise," replied Fina.

Fina paused and shifted on the bed. "I assume you didn't kill her."

A burst of air indicated Ruby had returned to the room.

"Ruby!" cried Fina, outstretching her arms as if this was their first reunion in years.

In a comic gesture, Ruby looked from Fina to Emeline and then back again. She shook her head in disbelief.

Fina was so focused on Ruby that she had scarcely a moment to see Emeline's face after she made her statement about the murder. That moment told her nothing. Emeline had resumed her rigid posture and slight pucker of her lips, as if she were perpetually sucking on a lemon.

"Ah, Fina, I'm glad to see you're feeling better. But why—" Ruby faltered. She flopped down in a chair. Fina couldn't help but notice that it was the farthest possible seat from Emeline.

Emeline rose from Ruby's bed. She clutched her carpet bag, strode to the door and said, "Thank you for our little chat, Miss Aubrey-Havelock. I will bid you adieu." And with that, she slammed the door.

"What in heaven's name?" said Ruby, still looking completely bewildered.

A little rush of pleasure at having vital information coursed through Fina's veins. "She's the contact!"

Ruby's eyes widened but then she shook her head. "Not possible, not possible."

"But she told me the code word – Wendell!" Fina proceeded to retell the rather miraculous story to Ruby. As she repeated the story out loud, it began to sound progressively unbelievable.

Ruby sat patiently and didn't interrupt. But Fina could tell from her face that she wasn't convinced.

As she finished her tale, Fina said, "I know it sounds rather preposterous, but it's so preposterous that it is believable!"

Ruby nodded. "You do have a point there, Feens. It would be hard to concoct a more half-baked story than that."

Fina lowered her head. "Then you don't believe it?"

"I didn't say that. I just said it is rather implausible," she sighed. "But, as we know from past experience, the implausible can be true."

Readjusting her pillows into a comfy backrest, Fina said, "Has something happened that makes you doubt Emeline's story? How is Agnes, by the way?"

Ruby smiled. "Agnes is unconscious, but Violet said she is likely to recover. Thank goodness."

Her smile turned to a frown. "As to the other question, I do doubt Emeline's story."

"Why?"

"Because Lev just pestered me again about those books Neville gave you."

Fina groaned. Was everyone on this ship their contact, starting with Victor and his pig?

"I know, Feens," Ruby said leaning back in her chair as if she had just finished a rather rich meal. "Lev approached me after I left Violet and Agnes in Emeline's room. He asked me if the two of us had enjoyed Neville's reading recommendations. I said they were gratifying, especially the Makhno book. I assumed he meant that one. Then he questioned me about the Ngaio Marsh book – *A Man Lay Dead*. I said it was also entertaining. He kept pestering me about Marsh, asking what I thought of the characters and the plot. He was clearly prompting me to say something specific."

"And this is when you suspected this conversation had something to do with Wendell," said Fina slowly putting together the puzzle pieces in her mind.

"Exactly. This conversation, combined with Neville's earlier enquiry about the books, made me wonder if we missed something in the books."

"But I read the Makhno, cover to cover. Nothing. I even removed some of the backing on the book to see if there was a hidden piece of paper."

"Would you take a look at *A Man Lay Dead*? It's on the night-stand next to you."

Fina opened the novel. She flicked through it. "Why the mystery book?"

"Because unlike your conversation with Neville about the books – plural – my conversation with Lev was about Marsh, not Makhno."

Fina flipped to the first page and began to methodically weave her way through the pages – not reading them, but looking for anything out of the ordinary. By the time she reached chapter four, she gave a little yelp.

Ruby hurried over to the bedside.

"Look!" squeaked Fina, pointing to the first page of the chapter. She read, "The <u>w</u>easel-like <u>e</u>yes of the <u>n</u>ew <u>d</u>on scanned the room with an <u>e</u>nterprising <u>l</u>ook. 'Look here,' he said."

Ruby began jumping up and down. "That's it, we've cracked it, Feens! Lev and Neville are the contacts."

After the initial excitement subsided, Ruby's jumping turned to pacing. "But how did Emeline find out about it, too? Why would she go to all that effort? And Lev and Neville had plenty of opportunities to make contact in much easier ways."

Fina nodded. "Someone must be lying."

"Or spying," said Ruby grimly. "We need to be careful who we trust."

32

Dinner was a pathetic affair. Everyone sat in their pairs that night – assuming their partner was still available, as it were. Even the food was lacklustre, but Fina knew how upset Sarah had been over the attack on Agnes. Before dinner was served, the captain announced they would arrive tomorrow afternoon. The thought of the authorities, the authorities coming on board and questioning... Fina shook her head. Worrying about it was not going to make it go away, she told herself firmly.

"Neville, will you please come here?" asked Gustave, sitting at a table with a rather sullen-looking Dolores. She stared into her glass of whisky. Fina admitted a grudging admiration for Dolores' tolerance of large quantities of alcohol. Sartorially, she looked marvellous, as always. Given her countenance, however, the large floral print evening dress and two-tone cape seemed to be wearing her, rather than the other way around.

Gustave licked his lips as he lifted his glass of wine to his mouth. His hand was shaking again. He certainly had a hearty appetite. Dolores kept offering him her untouched food, which he grabbed at with the look of a ravenous goat.

Sadie and Victor sat with Phillip and Gilbert. Emeline had

asked to eat her dinner in her cabin, which she had volunteered as a recuperation space for Agnes. It was deemed to be more comfortable than the staff quarters. Violet also joined them to keep a watchful nurse's eye on Agnes.

Both Sadie and Phillip had those pasted-on smiles with vacant stares which adults often use to pretend they're paying attention to a child. Fina could tell that Victor wasn't fooled. He didn't really seem to care as 'Wendell' made little snorting noises and ploughed through a pile of untouched peas on his plate. Clearly, his mother would have frowned on this activity if she had been paying attention. Gilbert was watching the older boy, and soon enough he, too, had a little sheep that was merrily leaping about on a bed of fluffy rice. Fina smiled at this playfulness amidst the gloom.

"What is going on in that brain of yours, Fina?" enquired Ian, not unkindly. "I can practically see those little grey cells dancing around inside your head."

Ruby leaned over and said in a fake-whisper, "That's Fina's special look. It happens when she is observing minute details with that photographic mind of hers. When she's got that look, I don't distract her because we often need those photographs for later!"

Fina smiled. Her friend knew her better than she knew herself. She had once pointed out to Ruby that she was going to wear through the rug in her little room at Oxford from all that pacing she did. Fina vividly – photographically, in fact – remembered Ruby staring down at her feet and then the rug in surprise. Then she had let out a great belly laugh, that rare departure from her usual giggle.

"There," Fina said, snapping her head around in a mechanical motion to look at Ian. "I've finished my photography session for the evening."

Ian put down his fork and pushed away his plate. "So, you two, what are we all going to do when tomorrow comes?"

"Thanks, Ian, for ruining any appetite I might have had," said Ruby, dabbing the corners of her mouth with the cloth napkin. Fina looked at Ruby. Oh no, she thought. But then Ruby's eyes crinkled at the corners, indicating she was not entirely serious.

"I'm well aware of our rather dire situation. And I really don't want to believe that anyone on this ship could have committed these crimes," said Ruby, shaking her head in resignation. Then she lifted her head higher. "But I am fairly certain I know who did it," she whispered.

Ian's eyebrows wiggled as he leaned in closer to Ruby. "Yes?"

"Don't be silly, Mr Clavering. I cannot tell you until I'm certain," she said. Then she gestured at Fina. "Look at Fina – she knows better than to pester me about it because it will make me even more stubborn about keeping it to myself. Stubbornness is a lovely, useful trait that Fina and I share."

Fina beamed. "Oh yes, it's quite true. I prefer to call it persistence rather than stubbornness," she said. Looking at Ian, she continued, "The person who keeps their tongue keeps their friends."

Ian leaned back and threw his hands up in mock surrender. "I see, I see. That's all well and good, but when do we get to hear the news? I don't know about you, but I'm awfully anxious about having to explain, ah, certain things, to the authorities."

"Tomorrow. I'll tell you tomorrow," replied Ruby.

"Don't tell me you're going to do that rather theatrical announcement game that you did last time," said Ian.

"Absolutely not."

Ian drew a line along his jaw with his index finger, ruminating. "On second thoughts, it might be the best way. After all, we'll have to make an announcement – or rather Maxwell will have to make an announcement – to the passengers before we leave. And it might help us all tie up some loose ends in our interviews with the authorities."

Ruby shook her head. "No, I'd rather not, because if word gets out among the passengers..."

"How about this? I'll tell Maxwell that you know – he will keep it confidential – and ask his opinion. If he says yes, then you'll do it?"

Ruby smoothed her hair and the dress material on her lap. Fina realised this was a technique that let her pause and think.

"I'll do it. After breakfast tomorrow. In the lounge."

33

It was a blue moon occasion: Fina didn't eat breakfast the next morning. Well, not a proper breakfast, she thought, as her stomach gurgled. Just plain toast and tea. She didn't know how Ruby could tuck away johnnycakes, eggs and bacon, and then wash it down with three cups of coffee. But it must be giving her much-needed strength for the looming tempest.

In addition to breakfast, they ran about preparing for Ruby's revelations. The captain had told the passengers that he expected to see them all in the lounge mid-morning.

"Ah, there it is," said Ruby, kneeling down to rummage in the back of a low cupboard. She pulled out a dusty white tin box with a red cross: a substantial first aid kit.

"Gracious, Ruby, what have you got planned?"

But Ruby only had time to make a reassuring gesture in Fina's direction before she dashed off in search of Neville, leaving the first aid kit on a side table. She'd told Fina to keep the passengers busy in the lounge while Neville gathered some items from their cabins, unseen. Then he was to bring this collection to the lounge.

Even as she chatted idly with the guests, something nagged at her. Ruby had looked for something in Balraj's room, something she'd said had been missing. Could she have sent Neville in search of it? But no, that couldn't be it – he'd been sent to collect something specific, not to launch a full-scale hunt. This is so infuriating, thought Fina. Ruby can be so infuriating. But then she realised that she could be quite infuriating too – and Ruby put up with her.

Ruby was the last to enter the lounge, by design. The comfortable chairs sat in a little semicircle, facing the bow. Fina congratulated herself on finally learning which was the bow and stern of a boat. Sunlight streamed in through the windows. The chairs were arranged so guests could not only look out over the bow, but also be subjected to some intense sunlight, illuminating their every movement, even the slightest flinch of guilt. That had been Fina's idea, and she felt rather proud of it, even though it was devious. But this was murder. Dolores had subverted her plan by donning her sunglasses. Tricky, thought Fina. Tricky, indeed.

The sunlight also had another effect. It was a beautiful day, but looked to be warmer than ever. Fina's own personal temperature comfort range was quite small, so she was already beginning to sweat as they took their places at the front of the semicircle. Lev shut the doors, increasing the temperature and humidity tenfold.

Captain Mills, immaculate in his white suit – no beads of sweat on his forehead – stood up from his chair as soon as all had been seated. Unlike everyone else present, he seemed to be enjoying himself.

Everyone was present, except for Lev, Neville, Agnes and the two boys. Lev was keeping an eye on things on the ship's bridge, Neville was fulfilling Ruby's request, and Agnes was still in Emeline's room. They had agreed that as she was on the mend, she would watch over the boys until she was needed in the lounge.

"Dear passengers," said the captain. "I will not provide you with a lengthy introduction, except to say that Miss Dove, Miss Aubrey-Havelock and Mr Clavering – as you all know – have been investigating these dastardly crimes on my ship. It is my understanding that conclusions have been reached." He paused. "It is in all our best interests, not only for safety reasons, that we know who the murderer is – assuming it is singular rather than plural."

Clearing his throat after his grammatical diversion, Mills said, "I expect full cooperation from all of you this morning, just as I have requested during the investigation. I know this is quite difficult for all of us. Or should I say difficult for some of us more than others," he said, scanning around the circle as if he could ferret out the culprit by just looking at them. With that, he took his seat.

"This is outrageous," said Sadie, rising from her chair. "My late husband was one of the foremost members of the House of Lords, I'll have you know, and he would never have countenanced such baseless accusations."

"Hear! Hear!" rejoined Phillip. "I may not be one of the gentry, but I am a British subject," he said in all seriousness. Fina saw Ian's lips twitch with amusement.

The captain rose again. "Please, please. We are on this ship, and when we are at sea, I set the rules for conduct." He paused. Fina was quite sure he couldn't help himself when he finished by saying, "And as a British subject, Mr Gibbs, I expect you to understand stiff upper lips."

"Thank you, Captain Mills," said Ruby, rising gracefully from her seat. Her posture conveyed she was prepared to answer difficult questions from a board of bank directors.

"I know this conversation is a painful one, but I am doing it at the captain's request. Miss Aubrey-Havelock and Mr Clavering," she said, gesturing to Fina and Ian, "will chime in at various points to ensure we all stay close to the matter at hand. I'm most grateful to them for their patience," she added, grinning sheepishly at Fina. Fina felt somewhat mollified by this acknowledgement.

"Let us begin with the murder of Mr Balraj Chadha. At first it seemed inexplicable. On this voyage, Mr Chadha was the life and soul of the party, a friend to everyone. However, once I became aware of a single, crucial piece of information, it was clear to me that almost everyone in this room had a reason for wanting him out of the way, as it were." She paused and let her gaze circle the lounge, chin high, to the silent admiration of Ian. Truly, reflected Fina, her friend had a flair for drama, whether she realised it or not.

"But I'll say more about that in a moment. For now, let's recount what happened the night of the murder," she said, nodding at Ian. She sat down and drained a large glass of water near her side.

Ian stood up and buttoned his blazer. "Here's what we know about that night. We all assembled for dinner at 6 o'clock."

He turned to Violet. "Mrs Gibbs." She looked up, startled from her task of rearranging the vase of flowers and the sugar bowl on the table. "You were in your cabin because you were not feeling well. Did you hear anything during that time? Even more importantly, did you leave your cabin?"

Violet's healthy glow from yesterday quickly turned into a sickly sheen. "I don't know what you mean, I, I..." She began to tremble.

"There, there, dear," said Phillip, patting her hand as if she were a small child. He began to jiggle his leg.

Good grief, thought Fina. She hoped her husband never condescended to her like that. If she ever got married, that is.

Clutching her handkerchief, Violet whispered, "I had my dinner tray in my room. Miss Gidge brought it to me at 6 o'clock, as I'm sure you've already confirmed," she said, looking toward a nodding Ian. "And then I didn't leave the cabin. Phillip and Gilbert returned shortly thereafter – after the pea and plantain debacle. I heard nothing."

Turning to Dolores, Ian said, "And now you, Miss Dominguez."

Dolores' face was maddeningly impassive, thought Fina, especially with the sunglasses. "As I've already told Ruby and Fina, I retired to my cabin at 6 with a headache. By 6:15, I had begun to fall asleep. A knocking noise awoke me at 6:45."

"Right," said Ian. "Miss Gidge told us that she left the tray at 6:45 after hearing no answer from Balraj's room."

Phillip interjected. "That means the murder must have occurred between 6:20 and 6:40," he said with a satisfied smile. But then his face looked perplexed. "But at that time everyone was in the dining room, apart from my wife. She didn't do it, so that leaves…"

Everyone turned to stare at Dolores. She remained tranquil. Ruby rose from her seat. "That does seem to be the logical explanation. But let's not leap to conclusions. In fact, it could have been Mrs Gibbs, but it wasn't. You see, there are too many unknowns here. For someone to murder him in just twenty minutes, it had to have been planned in advance."

Fina's fingers tingled. "But how could the murderer know that Mr Chadha would go to his cabin?"

"Exactly," said Ruby. "Our murderer could have seized an unanticipated opportunity on the spur of the moment, and followed him to his cabin to kill him. The problem is they simply wouldn't have had enough time to do it."

Emeline puckered her lips. "Well, *Miss Dove*, what does this mean then?"

"It means," replied Ruby, "that the murderer wasn't there."

"It means," replied Ruby, "that the murderer wasn't there."

34

Gasps rippled around the room.

"What in the holy mother's name do you mean?" asked Gustave, levitating above his chair. His face was hardly impassive now. Little flecks of spittle flew from his lips onto Dolores, who gently wiped them away with her handkerchief.

Neville entered at that moment, struggling under the weight of a box. He looked satisfied, but grim. Ruby nodded at him and smiled. He stood at the table outside the semicircle as if he were awaiting orders.

"Yes. The murderer wasn't there." Again, another murmur of voices around the room. Fina saw Ruby warming to her role. The dramatic reveal was still to come.

"You see," said Ruby. "We know Balraj died from a blow to the back of his head."

"And from our calculations, it had to be someone quite tall, or someone in heels," interjected Ian. Fina smiled to herself.

"Yes, and by what we found in the room, someone had not only moved the body, but had cleaned up after themselves. They would have needed to find cleaning supplies and dispose of them afterwards – all in twenty minutes," said Ruby.

"Well, then it had to be Miss Dominguez!" said Sadie. "She would be tall enough in heels, and she was the only one besides Violet who had the opportunity."

"It would seem that way, Lady Winchcombe-Twisleton, but we still encounter the old problem of this being an impossible murder in terms of timing."

"Is this drama necessary? Please get on with it, Ruby," said Emeline in a harsh voice. Ian flashed Emeline a warning look. She ignored him.

"It's Miss Dove to me, Miss Caulk. In any case," she said, returning to her previous subject, "it is quite necessary and you'll see why when we come to a conclusion."

She continued. "Let's leave the problem of the seeming impossibility of Mr Chadha's murder to the side for a moment. Consider the case of Patricia Burbage's murder."

Emeline blew her nose loudly in her handkerchief.

Ruby glanced at Ian. He nodded. "We know that Mrs Burbage was killed by cyanide in her glass of port."

"Good God man, stop stating the obvious," yelled Phillip. Fina had never seen the man so agitated before. He was normally such a good-natured, rather bland character. Now he was all fire and brimstone. What had changed?

Ian ignored the outburst. "While we know the cyanide was in the glass – and that any one of us could have put it there given the distraction of the cat in the kitchen – we didn't know if it had originally been poured into the bottle. We did find out afterwards that it was in the bottle and Mrs Burbage's glass, but not Ruby's."

Ian's voice rose. "At first, I thought the target was Miss Dove. But after our analysis, with the help of Mrs Gibbs," he said, nodding gratefully in Violet's direction, "we discovered that the target was indeed Mrs Burbage. Miss Dove might have been a secondary target: although there wasn't poison in her glass, there was cyanide in the port bottle."

"And Mrs Burbage had told us earlier that she thought someone wanted to harm her," added Fina.

"Exactly," said Ian. "Add to that the scorpion incident – which initially seemed either an accident or a warning to Miss Caulk – and we have a relatively clear picture of a build up toward Patricia's murder."

"What about Miss Gidge?" asked Dolores. "Poor woman. I'm quite glad she is on the mend."

Obligatory nods of agreement came from everyone in the room.

"Miss Gidge knew too much," said Ruby. "It took her a while, but she had access to clues that no one else had. She tried to get in contact with Fina and me before she was attacked. She was hesitant to express her suspicions, but I believe the second murder made her feel that she had to come forward."

"Unfortunately, the murderer found her before we could," said Fina.

Agnes wobbled into the dining room on a makeshift cane.

Victor and Gilbert trailed behind her. Sarah looked to Ruby who nodded in reply. Sarah rose and the pair trundled after her like little ducklings out of the room. Fina had seen Ruby and Sarah discussing their plan of action earlier. Ruby said she wanted Agnes' entrance to be a surprise.

Fina saw looks of pity on her fellow passengers' faces as Agnes lowered herself in a chair just outside the circle. Neville rushed over to put a pillow behind her back.

Agnes surveyed the crowd, her hand resting on top of her cane, looking like an ancient soothsayer.

"Thank you for joining us, Miss Gidge. I know that we are all relieved, with the exception of one of us, that you are on the mend," said Ruby. "Now," she said, gesturing to the crowd, "I hope that Miss Gidge will share what she knows about these two murders – and her own attempted murder."

"Shall I begin with Mr Chadha, miss?" asked Agnes, wincing from pain, though also clearly enjoying her moment in the limelight, thought Fina.

"Yes, please do."

"Right, miss." She took a long sip of water from the glass Neville had brought to her. "As you all know by now, I brought trays to Mrs Gibbs, Miss Dominguez and Mr Chadha that first night. The main thing is that I brought Mr Chadha's tray at 6:45, knocked and knocked but there wasn't no answer. So I left the tray thinking he'd fallen asleep. Course, when I picked it up the next morning, he hadn't eaten it, had he? That's when I knew something wasn't right."

"And that's when we discovered he was murdered," said Ruby.

"Right you are, miss. Awful it was, though there weren't much blood. I didn't think about it at the time because I never seen a murder before."

"What happened then, Miss Gidge?" asked Fina.

"Well, I went about my business, as usual. Though the whole thing made me nervy. Always looking over my shoulder, I was," she said, leaning back in her chair. "But after the second murder, some ideas in my head began to bother me more. It was like there was a bee buzzing in the back of my head. It wouldn't leave me alone, but I couldn't quite figure out where or what it was."

"And that was the key to the whole mystery," Ruby put in. "The clue that escaped us all, but which, if I'd only realised it, one of the ship's crew had known about all along."

She exchanged glances with Agnes, who nodded at her.

"The bed-clothing."

35

Fina glanced around at the crowd, feeling just as lost as most of them looked.

Agnes carried on nodding her head incessantly. "Yes, the bed-clothing, miss. You see, after the first murder, I was doing the wash as I always do. I count up the linens after they're clean. The pillows were all right, but one whole set of bedclothes was missing! I counted and recounted. I looked in the crews' wash. I even looked in the extra closets upstairs to see if they were there. Couldn't see hide nor hair of them. The only thing I could think was that a guest had put it in their luggage. But that seemed, well, daft."

"Why didn't you tell anyone then?" asked Fina.

"Well, miss, it was just too odd. I did ask the crew if they had seen any bed-clothing lying around, but they hadn't. I tried to ignore it, but it wouldn't let me be. That's when I slipped a note under Miss Ruby's door about wanting to talk to her," she said, nodding toward Ruby.

"And that's when you figured it out, Miss Gidge," said Ruby, quietly. "Your drawing on the note told me all I needed to know."

Agnes wiped her brow. "Yes, miss. You see, if I hadn't been there to see Mr Chadha's skull bashed in…" She paused. "Beggin' your pardon, ladies and gentlemen," she said with a little nod at the crowd.

"No need to apologise, Miss Gidge," said Ian. "That's what did indeed happen."

She gave Ian a little smile and continued. "Well, it was that problem of the blood. There should have been more, well, ah, blood and the like on the floor," she said, becoming squeamish at her own description of the murder. "And then the missing bed-clothing…" She trailed off with her hands in an open gesture, signalling that the guests should come to their own conclusions.

"I think you'd better walk us through your thought process," said Ruby.

"Right you are. Well, the reason for the lack of, ah, matter, could be that there was something catching that blood, or that Mr Chadha was killed elsewhere and the body had been moved. What if Mr Chadha had been killed either in his room or elsewhere – and then everything was cleaned up with bed-clothing? Certainly something would be needed to clean up that mess."

"That's why the rug was so clean in Balraj's room!" declared Fina, the truth beginning to dawn on her, ever so slowly.

"Exactly," said Ruby. "Either Balraj was killed and fell back on the bed-clothing, or the bed-clothing was used to clean up the mess. Though it seems more likely that he fell on the bed-clothing, because it would be impossible to clean the rug well enough – since the murderer was in a hurry."

"So this means that Balraj could have been murdered somewhere other than his own cabin," said Ian.

"Yes, sir," said Agnes.

"Wait a minute, Miss Gidge," said Sadie. "Wouldn't you have

noticed whose room was missing bedclothes when you cleaned the rooms? Then you would know the identity of the murderer!"

Agnes shook her head. "No, Lady Winchcombe-Twisleton. You see, I leave a note in all the guest rooms explaining that they can find extra linens in the cupboard near the reading room – at the stern of the boat. The murderer was clever and took extra linens from that closet. I counted them in that cupboard so that's how I know for certain one was missing."

"All well and good, but this just tells us what we already know," said Phillip. "It tells us that one of us is a murderer." His voice was increasing in volume yet again. Those Gibbses were peculiar, thought Fina. Distinctly peculiar.

"Yes, Mr Gibbs, that is exactly what it tells us," said Ruby in a calm voice. "It also tells us that the murderer wanted to kill Miss Gidge to suppress this knowledge." She looked sympathetically at Agnes.

"That's right, miss," murmured Agnes from her chair.

Ruby smoothed her hair and continued. "Since we've established that Miss Gidge's knowledge was clearly dangerous, let's review the reasons everyone had to murder Mr Chadha and Mrs Burbage."

"And which one was the *real* murder," said Ian, "assuming that one of them was the primary target."

"Mm-hmm," said Ruby, in between sips of water. "Let's start with the Gibbses, shall we?" She looked over to the fish-like countenances of the Gibbses. Violet grasped Phillip's arm so tightly that it looked as though her fingernails might pierce his skin.

Ruby glanced at Fina. Must be her turn.

"Ah yes, so perhaps you could tell us why you are travelling with a king's ransom in jewellery on this journey?" asked Fina, rather innocently.

"What?" said Violet. "What were you doing searching our room? What does that have to do with these murders?"

"It may have everything to do with them."

"Ah, I can explain, I can explain," said Phillip, chomping at his pipe. Fina couldn't tell if he was wincing from having to tell the truth or from his wife's vice-like grip. "To be frank, this trip is not entirely a pleasure cruise for us. Violet and I are planning to start a new life in Port of Spain. Sun, sea... it'll make a change from foggy old Blighty, eh, darling?" His laugh had a forced ring to it.

"If that's so, Violet," continued Fina, "why did I hear your husband say, 'Soon we'll be safe' to you?" continued Fina.

Violet looked at Phillip. Fina saw that she was clearly terrified.

Phillip coughed. "Very well, Miss Aubrey-Havelock, I see you hold all the aces. Jolly good. The fact is, we are on the run."

Well, well, thought Fina. He crumbled like a house of cards.

"You fool!" screeched Violet, slapping him across the face.

"On the run?" said Ian, incredulously. This pair did not fit his idea of professional crooks.

Tears streaming down her face, Violet said, "Let me explain. You see, we were afraid for Gilbert."

At least three people said in unison, "Gilbert?"

"Yes, Gilbert," said Violet. "And myself. You see, I was married when I was quite young. To a soldier in India. It was a washout. He went missing – and his friends believed it was related to his military service. Even though I wanted to break it off, I waited. And waited. Over two years. Then I left India and returned to London. I assumed he was dead, as did everyone else. I started a new life as a widow."

"Then I met Vi in London," said Phillip, wiping away Violet's tears. She gave him a half-hearted smile. "We married, and, a year after, Gilbert was born."

"We were quite happy," said Violet, blowing into her handkerchief. "Until a month ago, when I had a letter from a friend in India, telling me that my first husband was alive. Not only was he alive, but he was returning to London."

Phillip removed his pipe and began to wave it around. "Well, you all know the severe punishments for bigamy. Sometimes two years in prison. Gilbert would lose his mother. We thought the best plan was to escape, somewhere where no one could find us, nor would the news matter when Violet's, ah, husband returned to London. Violet has an aunt in Port of Spain, so that's how we decided on Trinidad. We left instructions with our families to tell the authorities that Violet had died and that I had vanished with Gilbert somewhere."

"So the jewellery was your life savings?" asked Fina.

"Yes," said Phillip. "We thought it would be the safest way to travel – convert all of our money into jewellery that could be easily sold anywhere."

"So that's why Mrs Gibbs has looked so ill during this voyage. The three of you never really seemed like you were on holiday," said Fina. Then she looked at Ruby. "What does this have to do with the murders?"

"Would you like to tell everyone or should I?" asked Ruby, looking at the pair.

Violet gave out a sigh that turned into a cough. "I'll tell you. We didn't think anything of it at first, but Balraj, Mr Chadha, that is, made subtle hints about my husband and marriage."

"At first I thought he was, well, making a pass at my wife, of course," said Phillip. Fina fought down her urge to judge that comment.

"But then we realised that he travelled quite frequently between India and England," said Violet. "And that his social circles might be abuzz with gossip of the sort related to subjects like..."

"Bigamy," whispered Phillip.

"Did you ever confront Balraj about it?" asked Ruby.

"No," said Violet. "But we did live in fear that he might tell someone."

Around the room, the silence of those listening took on a cold, hostile quality. Violet, realising that she had brought their suspicion on herself with her own words, shrank back into her chair and clamped her lips tightly shut.

Ruby turned back to the room. "Violet's fear was legitimate," she said in a clear voice. "Balraj Chadha had a talent for exploiting his knowledge of people's secrets. And exploiting those secrets for a great deal of money. But he wasn't pursuing people like the Gibbses. Strangely enough, he had principles – he only targeted those with money, prestige or power. And his secrets cost him his life."

36

———

Fina leaned back in her chair. Never mind a flair for drama, she thought; Ruby had a positive genius for it.

"I first realised the possibility that Balraj was an opportunist when Sadie mentioned it in a conversation," Ruby went on. "Soon after that, Gustave made a similar comment, though he did not provide any details about what kind of opportunism he meant."

Sadie shifted in her seat. Gustave, for all his impassivity, held his head high.

"I knew that Balraj was out of work because of his stand against discrimination in the film industry, so that led me to wonder where he secured the money to come on this trip. In hindsight, of course, the answer was obvious: money in exchange for silence."

Neither Sadie nor Gustave responded to this supposition. Ruby continued. "I do not know why or when he began these activities, but I can speculate on the matter. Anyone who knew him better than I is more than welcome to offer any additional information," she said, scanning the crowd as if anyone would actually take her up on this offer.

Silence.

"Given what little I've gathered about Mr Chadha's character from all of you, it seems unlikely that extortion was a natural expression of his personality. Far from it – he seemed to be a rather generous soul – and, at least in some ways, a very principled soul at that. It is my guess that he was short of money."

Dolores nodded and held up her finger as if she were a student waiting her turn to answer a question.

Ruby played along. "Yes, Miss Dominguez?"

"What you say is true. I think I was the closest of anyone to Balraj on this journey," she said, lifting her sunglasses to dab at her eyes. Was this all an act? It was rather convincing, even taking her profession into account.

"You see, after he took a stand against the stereotyped roles he played – and general treatment of his people in the industry – he was soon unemployed," Dolores continued. "He fell on hard times. Because he was an actor, and moved in high-class circles, he began to collect titbits of gossip and rumours about rich people. Rich people who controlled the film industry in England and the United States. He loathed them, so he thought he'd start asking them for money to keep their secrets quiet. Most of the time he had no firm proof that the rumours were true, but even rumours can bring down a wealthy person quickly in these days of scandal-mongering newspapers."

"And I'm sure the people whom he threatened knew that he would make good on his promise if they didn't give him money," said Ruby.

"Yes," said Dolores. "And then, well, something changed in him. He became hardened. I began to notice that he treated everyone – including me – like a potential enemy. I think he began to enjoy torturing wealthy people. No, enjoy isn't the right word," she said with a great sigh. "It wasn't pure enjoyment, but rather a game or a distraction for him, long after he had enough money."

"Which is how he could afford to sail to Trinidad," interjected Fina.

"He must have felt a sense of power," said Ian with a sympathetic yet rueful smile on his face. "All these people who decided his fate for so long now had to answer to him."

Ruby cleared her throat. "Yes, well, regardless of his own internal justifications and motives, the fact is that this behaviour, given how widespread it was, was going to provoke someone at some point."

"Not that it is an excuse for murder," said the captain.

"Quite," said Ruby.

The tears had never stopped streaming from Violet Gibbs' eyes. "But we never hurt him!" she wailed. "I never touched him! We just wanted to get away."

"Ruby, my dear," Gustave broke in, "this is all, as the British say, rather airy-fairy. Do you have a point to tormenting these poor people? I have some important letters to write before we arrive."

"Yes, my dear," said Ruby in a low voice. "There is a point. The point is that the Gibbses had a perfectly legitimate motive for murder and also had the opportunity – even given the impossibility of timing. Violet could have murdered him, gone back to her cabin and then when Phillip left with Gilbert, he could have gone back to clean up."

"And they could have murdered Mrs Burbage because she knew something, just like Miss Gidge," said Fina, feeling triumphant. Then a thought occurred to her. "But where would they have obtained cyanide?"

"Excellent question," said Ruby. "And one that we'll return to shortly. But as Mr Marchand has just spoken, let's explore his motives next."

Ian jumped up, ready to explain. "I knew there was a good reason for Gustave to murder Balraj. When I first met him, I began to think about how strange it was that he was a dress designer. He seemed – at least from the stereotypes in my mind – to be a more likely banker than a designer. It was also odd how he didn't want to talk about his life in France or in England, though that alone would not make me suspect him."

Ruby took over. "Then, early on in our trip, I read about an embezzlement scandal in a newspaper. I asked Ian about it and he said there had been a spate of high-level banking fraud cases in England, involving a number of foreign accounts. There were holes in Gustave's story that tallied almost exactly with the time-line of that particular crime."

"Based on Ruby's suspicions, I asked the captain to radio for more information about the scandal. Not anything elaborate, mind, but just what the papers had been saying," said Ian. "It didn't take much to put two and two together, and realise that the man we know as Gustave Marchand was in reality wanted by police in two countries for financial crimes. He was travelling under a pseudonym, in the guise of an up-and-coming dress designer, in the hope of escaping a jail sentence."

That must have been why Gustave didn't want to admit he had been in England long – and had avoided talking about his profession, thought Fina. She chided herself for not thinking more about those newspaper headlines, too.

"So you think I was a target for Balraj's extortion?" asked Gustave. He shrugged and then answered his own question. "I see no point in denying it – especially since you all already know that I'm on the run – because it is utterly plausible given what we know about him. But I would hardly kill him for it."

"Why not?" asked Dolores.

"Because, my dear, I could simply disappear elsewhere. My dress designs, you know..." His stony features relaxed into a half-smile. "I've always been interested in fashion, so it was no great stretch to slip into this new life. In fact, it has been a great pleasure. Balraj put all that at risk, but I had ample funds to keep paying him in the meantime. As far as extortion goes, he was quite reasonable, I assure you."

"What about the murder of Mrs Burbage?" asked Dolores.

"I had no motive for that killing, and as I said, I did not have a strong enough motive to kill Balraj," Gustave said, folding his hands in his lap as a message of finality about the matter.

Ruby pursed her lips. "Let us turn now to the other passengers," she said, looking at Sadie, who was twisting and twirling her jade necklace. "Lady Winchcombe-Twisleton, or Sadie Stiles, you inherited a large sum of money from your late husband's estate, is that correct?"

"I see no point in denying it. Everyone knows it's true," she said with a little flop of her head to the side.

"And is it also true that you enjoy being Lady of the Manor?" asked Ruby.

Sadie shrugged. "I don't see anything wrong with wanting to be part of a grand tradition of British aristocracy. However, I don't see that this has anything to do with the murders."

"Balraj knew something, didn't he, that would cause a scandal?" asked Fina quietly. "It had something to do with that paper in your room, though I couldn't quite figure out what it meant."

"I don't know what you're talking about," said Sadie, giving Fina a cold stare. She paused. "You are quite the snoop, aren't you?"

"You'd better answer the question," said Ian. "Or would you rather deal with the authorities when we arrive?"

Sadie rubbed one hand up and down her bare arm in a rhythmic motion. She looked alarmed.

"Mr Clavering. Is it really necessary to involve the authorities in my personal affairs?"

Ian fixed her with his trademark glare, which had never failed to subdue insubordinate directors in rehearsals. "You seem to forget, Lady Winchcombe-Twisleton, that we are dealing with two murders on this ship, and another attempt at one. Your personal affairs can no longer remain a secret."

"Very well." She sighed wistfully. "You may already know that my husband was in charge of a number of famine camps in India. Recently, I found out that the conditions at two of these camps were among the worst the British have run in India. Not only that, but he was leading nutritional experiments on people." She shuddered. "Truly awful, but there it is. I didn't find out until after he died."

"And Mr Chadha knew about this and was threatening to extort money from you as well," said Ruby.

"Yes," she said, turning to Fina. "That was the piece of paper you found in our cabin – it was the rations the British government used to figure out how much humans could live on per day."

Fina thought back to the paper, with its quantities of rice, potatoes and flour. "But it was only 60 grams. That's not much more than, let's see... two ounces," she exclaimed.

"Quite," said Sadie sadly. She shook her head. "The funny thing about it is that apparently the British have been engaged in committing atrocities in these camps for a long time – it was and remains an open secret. But this was particularly egregious. If it got out, it would be a major scandal given Lord Winchcombe-Twisleton's position as a former peer in the House of Lords and a humanitarian. It also implicated a number of other people in my social circles."

"So he hadn't asked for money yet – Balraj, that is?" asked Ian.

"The reason I gave him the cold shoulder that first evening at drinks was that he had approached me about it in London. It was one of the reasons I decided to go on this trip with Victor. I needed to get away and clear my head. That's why it was a shock to see him, because it seemed like he was following me."

"It's entirely possible that he was following you," said Dolores from the corner. "And I can only imagine how furious he was about your husband's involvement in the famine camp tragedy."

"But I would never have killed him. I didn't know Mrs Burbage, either. I would never risk something like murder, because Victor would lose his mother," she said, now moving her head around as if he were lost.

Violet leaned over and put a hand on Sadie's arm. "Don't fret, Lady Winchcombe-Twisleton. The two boys are safe – Miss Breeze is looking after them." Sadie gave her a surprised look in return, which then settled into a warm smile.

Ian cleared his throat. "I suppose I'm next. This will be brief. I have known Balraj for quite a while, but only as an acquaintance on the theatre circuit. There were rumours about his activities, but I never heard anything directly."

"And Mrs Burbage?" asked Ruby, playing along.

"I had never met Mrs Burbage before this voyage. Of course, I had heard of her, as one does in newspaper columns from time to time."

"It's true," Ruby confirmed. "Mr Clavering lacked any discernible motive for either crime." She paused. "Though that doesn't mean he doesn't have one."

Ruby couldn't help herself when it came to Ian, thought Fina.

"How about the captain and crew?" asked Phillip.

The captain made a shifting noise in his seat as if to signal he was ready to talk. "I can vouch for my crew. And as for myself, well, I did know Mr Chadha, but that was through Ian. I'd hardly commit murder on my own ship. It would be very hard to do because someone on the ship knows where you are at almost every minute of the day."

Neville stepped forward. "I can say that between myself, Lev and Sarah, we had no love lost for Mrs Burbage, who was rather difficult. If we murdered every passenger who was rude to us, however, we'd be out of a job fairly quickly."

Ruby signalled they accepted these stories by looking at Dolores next. "Miss Dominguez, would you prefer that I explain your motive or shall I do it?"

Dolores had drifted over to the drinks tray in the corner, where she was fixing herself a scotch. Fina saw the clock on the wall read 11.

As she walked slowly back to her seat, she said, "I will tell the story. There isn't much to tell, since it's in the newspapers – you probably all saw it," she said, making a sweeping gesture with her glass around the room. "I caused quite a furore because I told the truth about those scum executives," she said, nearly spitting her drink back into her glass. "They prey on young girls and their dreams. Why shouldn't I expose it?" she said defiantly.

"I certainly sympathise with your story, Miss Dominguez," said Ruby, looking quite sincere about the statement. "I am inspired by your courage. But that does not change the fact that it still made you a target for Mr Chadha."

"How so?" asked Dolores.

"You had not provided the names of the perpetrators of the crimes. And you have also effectively disappeared – no doubt for your own safety. If Mr Chadha had disclosed your location to the press, or even worse, to these executives, you could have been in danger. Your career is already in danger."

Dolores nodded. "Yes, I know, but you see, most of my scandal was already out in the open," she said, taking a swig at her tumbler. "And besides, Balraj and I – we – had a past relationship, if you know what I mean. He had a soft spot for me.

Even though he was, I guess you'd say, far-gone, I know he would never put me in physical danger. Besides, I was more afraid for him, as I hinted to you, Miss Dove, than I was afraid of him."

Fina could see that although Dolores was also escaping her scandal, she had adopted an almost wholly nonchalant attitude to the affair. Must be the drink.

Wrinkling her nose, Fina said, "Is that why I smelled your perfume in Balraj's room?"

Dolores stopped, mid-sip. She lowered her glass. Tucking her hair behind her ear, she replied, "Yes, Fina. Our relationship was already over, but I had to really end it."

Sadie's eyes flickered. "Now that you've unveiled all of our dirty laundry," she said, sneering at Ruby, "how about you and your gal-pal, Miss *Aubrey-Havelock*—" she pronounced it with an exaggerated British upper-class accent "—tell us your motives."

"Hear! Hear!" said Phillip.

The captain intervened. "I'm sure Miss Dove and Miss Aubrey-Havelock will explain. Please remember that I asked them to review these motives out in the open. They did not want to do it themselves."

Ruby gave the captain a grateful smile. "Thank you, Captain Mills. Please know that Mr Clavering, Fina and I had to be convinced to do this. We don't like airing other people's 'dirty laundry' – as you say, Lady Winchcombe-Twisleton – any more than the rest of you," she said. Then her voice became louder and firmer. "And the fact is that one of us is a murderer, so it would make sense for you to save your vitriol for them."

The crowd looked mollified, but still unconvinced.

"I have no motive," said Fina. "I didn't know anyone, except Lady Winchcombe-Twisleton, Ruby and Ian before this journey."

"Thank you, Fina. As for me," said Ruby. "I knew Gustave,

and obviously Fina and Ian, before this voyage. I had heard of Mr Chadha, but not met him before – nor had Fina."

"What if he was bilking you as well?" asked Phillip. "How do we know you're not lying?"

Ruby gave Phillip a wan smile. "You don't."

37

"This is utter balderdash," said Emeline, who suddenly advanced toward the door. On her way, she pointed a shaking finger at Ruby. "As Mr Gibbs points out, you – you could be setting up this elaborate charade as a ruse! It wouldn't surprise me."

The captain stood up. "Please, Miss Caulk, take your seat again," he said, waving her back.

"As I said, you don't have any reason to believe me – or really anyone else. But we do have evidence that we shall present in a moment," Ruby said, regaining her composure after the small mutiny that had just threatened to erupt. "But first," she said, turning to Emeline, "we need to finish our review of motives. You are the last one on the list."

Emeline gulped and clutched her carpet bag.

"In Emeline's case, it might be better to focus on the second murder, that of Mrs Burbage," said Ruby. "You see, Fina and I know Emeline had a motive to kill her sister."

Gasps from around the room. Fina held her breath. While she knew Ruby would not reveal Emeline's possible connection to Wendell, would she reveal Emeline's pulp fiction secret? Jack Juliano unveiled? Surely not.

"Yes, it is horrible to contemplate, but it is possible. We heard that your sister threatened to cut off the money to your pet causes," said Ruby.

Strained sounds gurgled up from Emeline's throat.

Ruby held up a hand. "Even if that were not the case, you also had a motive to kill Balraj because we also heard that he had made your sister one of his victims. If he'd done that, your funds would most certainly be cut off."

Well, that was a risk, thought Fina. She knew Ruby was bluffing. It might be true, but they didn't know it for certain.

Emeline sighed. "What you say is true. He was extorting funds from my sister for some rather, ah, dubious liberties she took with her business. But I'd hardly kill him for that. Especially if my sister was going to cut me off, as you say."

Ian jumped in. "But if this story is true, it fits together perfectly. You kill Balraj to stop the extortion and then you kill your sister so you inherit the money!"

Everyone shifted in their seats to look more closely at Emeline. Fina had to confess that Ian was right. It did seem to fit together perfectly.

Emeline cleared her throat. "I admit it is rather convincing, except for one fact."

"What's that?" asked Phillip.

"I inherit nothing under my sister's will," she sighed. "You see, that row we had about my *causes*, as you call them, was because I wouldn't inherit anything from her will. In fact, the only money I received from her was an allowance."

Ian looked disappointed as he sat back in defeat. "I see. Yes, that does seem to eliminate your motive."

Rustling sounds emanated from Neville's table.

Ruby gave Neville and his crate of surprises a slight nod.

He unpacked it slowly, clearly enjoying the theatricality of the moment.

"What on earth?" said the captain, staring. All eyes were on Neville now – in his striped sailor shirt. Much better than that stiff uniform, thought Fina.

Neville reached into the box and pulled out an object, then another, placing each one on the table. He handled them with great care, as if the stone might shatter.

"Those are the statues from our rooms!" declared Sadie.

"Yes," said Ruby, strolling toward the collection of figures. All eyes followed her, like a minute hand on a clock. She picked one up. "You see," she said, smoothing her hand along the parrot's wing, "these are sandstone parrot statues. Neville carved them all himself."

"Yes, I did. They're nearly identical. But not quite."

"Did you notice anything odd when you collected them today from all the guest rooms?"

"No, Miss Dove. They were all there, in their right places. I attached a label to each one showing where it came from – which cabin, that is." He handed over a statue to Ruby, with a paper tag tied around its neck.

Ruby held up the statue to the crowd, rather like a magician displaying an empty top hat, thought Fina. The rabbit was due any minute.

"Some of you may know," she said, her voice carrying clearly in the silence, "that my field of study at Oxford is chemistry. It's an interesting study in itself, but where it really becomes fascinating is when it may be used in real-life applications." She paused. "Such as catching a murderer."

All eyes followed her as she turned to the first aid kit and opened it. They seemed hypnotised. Fina wasn't sure she could have spoken, even if Ruby had asked her to. Neville, meanwhile, was arranging the parrot statues in a neat row along the table.

Ruby took out a small, brown glass bottle and some cotton wool. Again, she held up the bottle. "Ordinary hydrogen peroxide, such as you'd find in any first aid kit. It's a useful antiseptic and is excellent for disinfecting a needle, say, if you need to get out a splinter. That's because it reacts with blood, which contains an enzyme that breaks down the hydrogen peroxide into water and oxygen."

A voice spoke up. It was Dolores, perhaps emboldened by her drink. "Ruby, darling, this is all very impressive and I'm sure your chemistry skills are just as well-honed as your dressmaking ones. But are we not wasting time? If one of those statues was covered in blood – and surely it would have been, if it were the murder weapon – Agnes would have noticed, don't you think?"

"Would she?" said Ruby quietly. "Let's find out."

She opened the bottle and saturated a blob of cotton wool with hydrogen peroxide. Its sharp, medicinal odour drifted out across the assembled company, clashing with the soft comfort of the lounge.

Confidently she took up the first statue and swept the cotton wool evenly over the top of its head. The crowd held their breath. Nothing.

Ruby placed the statue to her left. One down, seven to go, thought Fina.

As the row of statues to her left grew, a nervous restlessness permeated the room. The earlier stillness was gone, replaced by a constant shuffling of feet, crossing of arms and clearing of throats.

The fifth statue looked exactly like the rest. But when Ruby swept her fresh ball of cotton wool over its head, Fina gasped. The clear liquid from the bottle foamed up instantly, turning a fizzy white everywhere it touched the stone.

It was what they had all been waiting for. Ruby set the statue down carefully and examined the label. "The murderer thought they had cleaned their statue thoroughly," she announced. "But sandstone is porous. You might wash away all visible marks, but no amount of soap and water could remove every trace of blood. This is the statue that killed Balraj."

The captain leaned forward. "And which cabin did it come from?" he asked.

"Mr Marchand's cabin," she replied.

38

Waves lapped against the boat. They sounded so loud, thought Fina, in the absence of human voices.

Fina had heard of people turning purple and grey – indeed she had seen it herself – but up until now she had never seen someone actually become green. That shade crept up Gustave's face, threatening to engulf his rapidly disappearing hairline.

Tick-tock. The grandfather clock chimed. If she listened carefully, she could hear squeals of laughter, children's laughter – must be Gilbert and Victor, she thought.

Gustave rose and then fell back into his chair. Though Fina thought the colour on his face might indicate impending apoplexy, he said in a steady voice, "It's a – what do they say in films? A frame-up. You," he said, pointing to Neville, "or you," pointing to Ruby, "put that statue in my cabin – or one of you!" he said, his finger moving rapidly from one passenger to the next.

Ruby shook her head. "I'm afraid not. You see, after Mr Chadha's death, the captain instructed all of us – even more so after Mrs Burbage's murder – to keep our doors locked. There wasn't an opportunity to switch the statues."

Trying another tack, Gustave asked, "This still doesn't prove anything. What does it have to do with the murder?"

"Booby trap," declared Ruby.

A little nest of baby squirrels awoke in Fina's stomach. Of course! A booby trap.

"I, I, I don't know what you mean," stammered Gustave.

"Of course you do," said Ruby. "But I will spell it out. The night of Mr Chadha's murder, you arranged to meet him in your cabin to discuss his terms – about the money he wanted from you. You gave him these instructions: during dinner, he should say he didn't feel well and then go to your cabin, not his own. He did this. You told him you'd leave it unlocked. You also told him that you would follow behind quickly. You didn't follow through on your promise, however, because you knew you didn't have to."

"Because Balraj would have already been dead," said Ian, staring at the sea.

Ruby continued. "You put this statue, perhaps along with some other heavy items as insurance, on the top ledge over your cabin door on the inside – the same one we all have in our cabins. I'm not sure what material you used – probably sewing thread. You'd have plenty of that as a dress designer. Then you closed the door and rigged the handle with the heavy objects above so they would come crashing down on whomever came in the door to your cabin. Then you must have crawled out through the window of your cabin and proceeded to go to dinner."

Dolores said, "But wait! Wouldn't the door be open after everything fell on top of him? Then anyone passing by Gustave's cabin would have seen Balraj."

"An excellent point. It bothered me for quite a while, but I realized Gustave must have arranged it so the trigger point would have been the closing of the door shut, not just the motion of opening it," said Ruby, taking a sip of water.

As it all began to come together, Fina said, "Then Gustave must have gone back to his cabin – after he and Ian had a nightcap in the green room."

Ruby shivered. "Yes. That was the first thing that struck me as incongruent, though it took me quite a while to realize it. Do you remember the conversation I had with Gustave at dinner the night of the murder, Fina?"

Fina could feel her brow furrow in the effort of remembrance. "Didn't you suggest that the two of you could sketch together that evening after dinner?"

"Exactly. Gustave replied that he was too tired. I took that at face value at the time. Not only should it have been a hint about his original career – given his rather weak sketching skills, but also—"

Ian jumped up. "He went to have a nightcap with me in the green room instead. And he was the one who made the suggestion!"

"Right. While it could have been that he was looking for an excuse not to sketch with me, which was odd since that's exactly what we're supposed to be doing on this trip, why would he suggest a nightcap with Ian?"

Fina's frame bolted upright into a ramrod straight posture. "He didn't want to return to his room because he'd have to sit with a corpse until the middle of the night!"

Ruby gave Gustave a sympathetic look. "It must have been awful to have to wait with the body in your room until, what, 2 o'clock in the morning? Isn't that right, Gustave?"

Gustave's face had returned to its frozen state. No reply.

"Then you must have dragged the body – I surmise you used a dressmaker's bag or some sort of item to hide it – just past Dolores' door to Mr Chadha's cabin. By then, you had his key, since it was in his pocket. You didn't stand much chance of being caught. Luckily for you, there was a storm. You also had an advantage because you only had to go a very short distance. Though you did have to push aside the untouched dinner tray that had been left for him."

Dolores eyes widened. "That must have been the sound that woke me at two in the morning?"

Ian and Ruby both nodded at her.

"What about the bedding?" asked Fina.

"He must have thrown those overboard," said Ian. "They were underneath Balraj when he was killed to catch any of the... mess."

"But why not throw the statue overboard?"

"Its absence would have been noticed, I expect," said Ian, "by Agnes, if no one else. He felt safer keeping everything the way it was before."

"Wait a minute," said Fina, recalling their first search of Balraj's cabin. "I've just realized that the statue was missing from his desk the first time we looked in his cabin. Why was Balraj's statue missing if Balraj was killed with Gustave's statue?"

"Yes, I was puzzled about that, especially because the statue miraculously reappeared the second time we searched his cabin," said Ruby.

"I know," said Ian, his eyebrows wriggling furiously. "Gustave must have taken it when he first moved the body so he could have a 'clean' statue appear on his desk – in case anyone became suspicious. This gave him time to scrub the murder weapon clean. Once that was accomplished – and it must have been quite a job to scrub it clean – he returned Balraj's original statue to his room and put his own statue, the murder weapon, back on his own desk."

"But why not switch the statues? In other words, wouldn't it be safer to put the murder weapon back in Balraj's room so it couldn't be traced back to himself?"

Ruby smoothed her hair. "Yes, that's what was just puzzling me right now after our little experiment, but I suspect it was to be on the safe side."

"Safe side?" asked Fina.

"Yes, he couldn't be sure that the statues were identical – after all, they were hand carved by Neville, so there were bound to be small differences. It's unlikely anyone would have noticed, but he didn't want to take that chance."

Everyone began to move their heads up and down as if the truth were dawning on them slowly.

Phillip asked, "What about Mrs Burbage?"

"As we already established, Gustave suspected that Patricia knew that he was under pressure from Balraj. That was confirmed by the séance and the revelation about money. Little did Gustave know that there were other extortion victims on the ship. He was sure that she would figure out what had happened. It's the same story for Miss Gidge."

Agnes coughed. "Yes, Miss Dove. You see, I asked all the guests if they had any extra linens to be washed – as I was missing a set. It was an innocent question. I asked everyone, you see, but he must have thought I was asking him especially."

"But how did he get the cyanide?" asked the captain.

Gustave cleared his throat. He folded his hands over his stomach as if he had just enjoyed a rather indulgent meal. He appeared strangely satisfied.

"Let me start by saying," he said, looking toward Agnes, "that I am truly sorry for what I did to you, Miss Gidge. I actually did not want to kill you – just incapacitate you. And I hoped that you might forget what had happened."

He turned to Ruby. "And to you, Ruby. I'm also sorry. I did try, rather clumsily, to poison your breakfast. But it was just like

Miss Gidge – I didn't want to kill you – just incapacitate you. And as for the port, I did put it in the bottle as well as Patricia's glass when everyone was distracted by the commotion in the kitchen. I did that after your port had been poured."

Ruby looked nonplussed. "Why?"

"Mainly to cause confusion," admitted Gustave. If everyone thought you were the intended target, they might not make the connection with Patricia's little séance." He sighed, as if overcome by the extent of his own deviousness.

"But as for the other two murders, I'm not sorry," Gustave continued, watching everyone's faces as they contorted into countenances reflecting puzzlement and disgust.

"Everything you say is true, Ruby," he said. "You are an excellent detective, as well as a dress designer. As for the cyanide, well, let me explain. All of you might be thinking right now that although I had a motive to murder Balraj, and then murder Patricia to hide my motive, you suspect my original motive not strong enough for murder."

He wiped his brow, but Fina noticed that his hands didn't shake.

"There is something that even you, Ruby, have failed to guess," he said with a small, tight smile. "For a long time now, I've been very ill. About six months ago, I found out that I had a year to live. A month or two ago, Balraj began to increase his payment demands. I simply couldn't keep up, and to make matters worse, he said he was tiring of this game. He threatened to expose me in London. If he had followed through on his threats, I would have gone to prison immediately while awaiting trial. My last months of life would be spent in prison."

The nervous tension began to ease off. Fina watched as the passengers' facial expressions softened a bit.

"I didn't know Balraj was going to be a fellow passenger on this voyage," he said, looking pointedly at Sadie. That must have been why she seemed so surprised at Balraj's appearance that first evening, thought Fina. She didn't know it, either.

"I think he rather enjoyed following his victims," he continued. "I was on the run, as it were, to beat the clock before I died. I thought I could spend my few remaining months in Trinidad. Lying in the sun."

Every muscle in Gustave's body relaxed. He melted into the chair. "As for Patricia. Well. I think she concocted that séance fiasco to find out if others had also had money extorted from them by Balraj."

"She saw your face during the séance," put in Ian. "She must have thought you were also a victim and therefore the murderer."

"Yes, when the planchette spelled out that horrible word, our eyes locked. In that moment, I could tell she knew I had also suffered the same fate. After that, I was afraid she'd give me away," he sighed. "Little did I know that Patricia and I weren't the only ones," he added, looking around the room.

"Did you put Souse, the cat, in Sarah's kitchen to create that awful fuss?" asked Agnes.

Gustave gave a slight affirmative nod of his head.

"What about the cyanide?" Phillip queried.

"Before I left England, I procured cyanide capsules for the time – when it came – for me to take my own life. I didn't know I would use them for other purposes."

He gazed around the room, legs crossed, his expression by now almost benevolent. It was a rather relaxed attitude for someone confessing to murder, Fina thought.

Gustave reached into his waistcoat pocket with a limp hand. Ian tensed visibly. Lev and Neville leapt to their feet. But when Gustave pulled out his hand, all it held was a tiny pill. He popped it into his mouth and smiled.

"Do not torment yourselves. Goodbye."

39

"Do you think we could fly back to London?"

Ruby sipped her orange drink and considered Fina's question. She gave her a slow smile. "I know what you mean. I've certainly had enough sea travel to last me quite a while."

Fina settled back in her chair to enjoy the scenery. Here they were in a seaside cafe, without a care in the world. Well, almost.

"But the problem is we lack funds, Feens. I asked Captain Mills if we might work on his ship to fund our way home, after we stop in St Kitts. He said he'd see what he could arrange," said Ruby.

"Ah well," said Fina. "The main thing is that we enjoy the time we have here," she said, slurping a spoonful of ice cream. She sat up. "But before we plunge into full relaxation mode, I do have a few questions for you. Then I promise I won't ask you again."

"Fair enough! What do you want to know?"

Fina rubbed her temple as if that would help her remember all the loose ends she wanted tied up after that terrible day Gustave had killed himself. Fortunately, the authorities had understood the situation quite quickly and there was minimal fuss.

"First of all, what about the scorpion in Patricia's bed? That can't have been Gustave; he had nothing to fear from her then."

"Yes, I did forget about that. I have an inkling that it may have come from a little closer to home."

"What do you mean?"

"Believe it or not, I think Emeline did it herself."

Fina grabbed Ruby's arm. "Crikey," she said in a low voice. "You cannot be serious! Why would she do a thing like that?"

Ruby also lowered her voice, even though there was no one within earshot. "Emeline's double life has put her under a lot of pressure. She's had no one to confide in, no one who can understand what she's gone through. Presumably that love affair she mentioned to you didn't have a happy ending. When that all ended, she was left with a companion who bullied her mercilessly and humiliated her in public."

"Of course," breathed Fina. "Poor Emeline must have been under great strain."

"And Patricia kept a tight hold on the purse strings, too – another way to assert her dominance over her sister. I think Emeline's little bouts of mischief-making were part of a long-running campaign to undermine Patricia, and get revenge for the way she was being treated."

"So she was responsible for the other threats and near-misses, too?"

Ruby nodded. "No doubt. I don't think she actually meant to kill her sister, but she hoped to rattle her. She managed it very carefully so that it would look like some third party bore a grudge against Henry, which was then transferred to his widow. Patricia was completely taken in."

Taking a last sip of her drink, Ruby said, "You know, I hope

Emeline continues with her work for our cause. With skills like that, she'll make a very effective operative."

A waiter materialised with another tray of delicious drinks. Fina selected a blue one this time.

She settled back into her chair. "So she turned out to be the contact after all? In all of the chaos around the murders, we haven't been able to discuss it. Did you give her the letter from Wendell?"

"Dear Feens, you are so patient with me. I was completely distracted by the events of the past few days. I did give it to her, though not without checking her credentials very thoroughly. She really had the perfect disguise. A little too perfect for me, if you know what I mean," she said, one corner of her mouth lifting a little.

Continuing on, she said, "After I gave Emeline the letter, she returned the favour with one that I was to deliver to our contact. That part was quite easy to arrange as soon as we arrived here."

A shadow fell over Fina's face, providing welcome relief from a sharp ray of sunlight.

Ian.

Fina sat up straight, bracing herself for the impact of his arrival.

"I see you two have the right idea," he said, toasting them with his own glass of water.

"Would you like to join us, Ian?" asked Fina, seeing no way to avoid the invitation.

Ruby shot her a look. She knew that look.

"Thank you, but I have an appointment. Just wanted to see how the two of you were getting on..." he drifted off.

"As you can see, we're quite well, thank you," said Ruby, not removing her sunglasses even though she was staring at him.

"I see. That's how you feel," he said with a smile and a shrug.

Ruby's shoulders slumped. Fina couldn't tell if it was

genuine emotion or the scenery that broke through her wall of defiance.

"Are you in Port of Spain for long?"

"Just for a few days. I may visit an aunt in Grenada."

"When are you returning to London?"

"I'm not sure. I have some things I need to sort out."

"Will you send me a postcard?"

"By all means," he said, shrugging again as if the request for something so prosaic as a postcard was the ultimate blow to his ego.

Ruby removed her sunglasses. "I mean it, Ian."

Looking mollified, he replied, "Of course, Miss Dove. You can expect a veritable avalanche of Royal Mail upon your return to the metropolis."

"I look forward to it."

Ian nodded and turned as if to go, but his disconsolate posture sparked something in Fina. It seemed a shame to part on such a cold, formal note. Without thinking, she burst out, "Ian, we were just discussing the trip, and how remarkable it was – for all the wrong reasons. But of course, you had your own task to fulfil, didn't you?"

There was no reply, but Fina thought she caught a hint of a smile. Emboldened, she pressed on.

"Did you manage to complete your, er, mission? Now, what was it again?"

Ian could no longer restrain himself, and he broke out into a grin. "Miss Aubrey-Havelock, your talents as an investigator know no bounds. One would hardly know one was being pumped for information. And, since my mission, as you call it, is now over and done with, I believe I can fill you in, as the Americans say."

He leaned casually against the back of Ruby's chair.

"Well, there are certain parties in my circle who are keeping a very close eye on developments pertaining to underground revolutionary networks. There's more activity on that front than you might think."

"Why, I am shocked by this unexpected news," said Ruby, drily, even though there was a twinkle in her eye.

Ian went on, ignoring her irony. "There were two people on the ship who we think play a role in one of those local networks. My job was to keep an eye on them."

"Who?" gasped Fina, no longer able to keep silent. "Not the Gibbses, surely?"

"No, not a passenger. It was Lev and Neville."

Fina sat back in surprise. She couldn't help noticing that Ruby didn't react at all. "I hope they're not in trouble?"

"Not in the least," replied Ian. "They never even knew they were being watched. One day, perhaps, I'll be at liberty to say more. In the meantime, I'll leave you two to your colourful drinks. Enjoy your time here," he said and strolled off along the water.

"Well!" said Fina, watching him go. "There is certainly more to that man than meets the eye. But Ruby, you don't seem a bit surprised. Was it because of the Makhno and Marsh code books, and the way they marked the Wendell code name?"

Ruby removed a small blue envelope from her bag. She slid it across the table to Fina. "Open it," she said. "Lev gave it to me as we disembarked the SS *Sanguine*." Then she leaned back in her chair and stared at the clouds while Fina began to read.

DEAR RUBY AND FINA,

Please destroy this letter after you read it.

We would like to explain our peculiar behaviour on this voyage, and how we came to know Ruby's brother's name. The Caribbean is a smaller place than you might think – especially among sailors. We met Ruby's brother on a voyage similar to this one, though this time it was from Nassau to St Kitts. It soon became clear that the three of us had much in common, politically speaking. This came up in our discussions of why Lev left Ukraine.

Though it was never discussed, we had the sense that Ruby's brother was actively involved in similar campaigns as us – and he had mentioned he had a sister at Oxford. When we saw Ruby's name on the passenger manifest, we wanted to try to see if she, too, had similar leanings. We cannot divulge any secrets in this letter. We thought you two could be helpful in our campaign. That is why we made that rather clumsy attempt with the books. All of our plans to make further contact with you were derailed by the murders.

Thank you for the opportunity to explain ourselves.
In solidarity,
Lev and Neville

FINA FOLDED up the paper and handed it back to Ruby. Ruby began to methodically tear up the letter into tiny, symmetrical strips. She then glanced at Fina.

"Well, I suppose that explains our rightful confusion. I hope we can come up with better code names in the future."

"When I tell Wendell this story, I'm sure he'll feel the same way!"

Fina lowered her sunglasses on the bridge of her nose. She stared at Ruby. Ruby returned the gesture.

"But this doesn't explain how someone else knew our code name, too," said Fina.

"Who?"

"Victor! Or, more precisely, his pig," said Fina.

Ruby winced. "I had forgotten about that, too. Do you want to hear my theory?"

"Please – I'm completely stumped," said Fina.

"Remember dinner that second night? The night of the first murder? In his rather irritating adenoidal voice, Gilbert repeated something about the open *window*. His adenoids caused it to sound like 'Wendell'. At least I think that's what Victor heard. Thus he was inspired to name his new pig *Wendell*."

"You are brilliant. And Wendell isn't that uncommon a name," replied Fina.

"And that pig did have a rather devious glint in its eye – making it a perfect namesake for a wily character like my brother!" said Ruby with a grin.

BONUS MATERIAL

The Mystery of Ruby's Smoke

Creating relationships with my readers provides fuel for the mystery-writing fire. To keep that going, I would love to keep in touch with you through occasional updates (no spam) via email.

As a thank-you gift for signing up, I'll send you special bonus material. Join the list and download the material by emailing me at rose@rosedonovan.com.

ENJOYED RUBY'S PORT?

The Mystery of Ruby's Port is the second book in *The Ruby Dove Mystery Series*. The first book, *The Mystery of Ruby's Sugar,* is available on Amazon.

I'm looking to you, dear reader, to share your views about this series. Reviews online are wonderful and word of mouth is even better.

If you enjoyed this book, I would be grateful if you spent a few minutes leaving me a review on Amazon.

Thank you!

ABOUT THE AUTHOR

Rose Donovan is a lifelong devotee of cozy mysteries. *The Ruby Dove Mystery Series* is her first foray into fiction, though she has written numerous non-fiction articles unraveling the mysteries of politics and injustice. Her next book in the series, *The Mystery of Ruby's Smoke,* will be released summer 2018.

Sign up to receive a thank-you for signing up and an occasional newsletter at www.rosedonovan.com.

www.rosedonovan.com
rose@rosedonovan.com
Follow me on Bookbub

NOTE ABOUT BRITISH STYLE

Readers fluent in US English may believe words such as "fuelled", "signalled", "hiccough", "fulfil", titbit", "oesophagus", "blinkers", and "practise" are typographical errors in this text. Rest assured this is simply British spelling. There are also other formatting differences in terms of spacing and punctuation, including periods after quotation marks in certain circumstances.